From close by in the forest came an eerie cry followed by a yapping chorus, and out of the trees at the edge of the gravel swept a little band of dark horses attended by a howling pack of what Michael Karl first thought were dogs. And then he saw more clearly—they were wolves!

The riders were an uncanny mixture of wolf and man, masked completely by shaggy gray wolf skins drawn over the upper parts of their bodies. They cantered silently down upon the train in dead quiet except for the excited yelps of their four-footed companions, whom they kept in order with long whips.

Black Stefan had come!

ANDRÉ NORTON

THE PRINCE COMMANDS

TOR

A TOM DOHERTY ASSOCIATES BOOK

The Prince Commands

Copyright © 1934 by D. Appleton-Century Company, Inc.; copyright renewed 1962 by Andre Norton

A Tor Book

Published by Tom Doherty Associates, 8-10 W. 36th St., New York, N.Y. 10018

First printing, March 1983

ISBN: 0-523-48058-X

Printed in the United States of America

Distributed by Pinnacle Books, 1430 Broadway, New York, N.Y. 10018

Author's Note

Once, some few years ago, a boy begged a story of me. It was to be of "sword fights and impossible things." I complied as best I could with this imaginary tale of Courts and Castles, Crown Princes and Communists. The telling of it was not in days, or weeks, but in months. However, I fulfilled my promise.

Here, *John*, is your story of "impossible things."

Chapter I

Michael Karl Learns What He Has Wanted To Know

"D'you know," Michael Karl flicked the chin of the boy in the mirror lightly with the thong of his riding crop, "d'you know that you're an awful disappointment and rather a failure?"

He attempted a stern frown but only succeeded in wrinkling his smooth forehead and twisting his level black eyebrows almost together.

"Oh, I know, m'lad, you can stick on a horse and know which end of a saber one holds. And I'm not denying that you can shoot at least decently straight and can order a breakfast in French. Nor do I forget that you can't remember tons and tons of European history which you've learned. But—Michael Karl—you, an American, don't know a thing about America, the country you live in. And you're a bit of a coward into the bargain."

The boy in the mirror dropped his gray-green eyes, and his thin lips became very straight indeed. Without looking at him again, Michael picked up his gloves and started for the door, his spurs rasping on the polished floor.

"Yes," he repeated, "you're a coward; you're afraid of your guardian and he but a man like yourself. No, not like yourself," Michael Karl sighed at his lack of inches and thought regretfully of the Colonel's six feet. The Colonel, that grim man, was the only family Michael Karl had had since his parents had been killed a month after his birth.

He straightened up to the last inch of his five-feet-six. It was his abiding misfortune that he was small, not short but small. He always had difficulty in getting gloves and boots to fit his long-fingered hands and high-arched feet and his clothes had to be made to order.

"Look at Napoleon," he comforted himself aloud, "I can imagine that a lot of people wished *him* smaller than he was."

But his lack of inches didn't produce his awe of the Colonel, at least he thought it didn't. As he was wondering whether it did, he opened the front door.

Outside, where a harum-scarum March wind was frolicking with the gardener's neat piles of last year's leaves and flower packings, he lost his soberness. He even attempted to whistle as he stood waiting for the groom to bring his mare around.

For yesterday Michael Karl had had an adventure and to-day he was calmly planning to have another, all without the knowledge of the Colonel. And adventures were something Michael Karl had read about rather than experienced for the past eighteen years.

The Duchess came dancing around the drive

from the stables with Evans at her haughty head. She had a wicked eye that morning, had the Duchess, and she promised some fun.

"She do be that flighty, sir." Evans was puffing a little. Her Grace had led him a merry dance.

"So I see." Michael Karl mounted. He had always wondered how heroes of romance "vaulted into the saddle." Some day when he had lots of time he would try it.

"Please, sir, will ye be a-lettin' me go with ye?" The Colonel, he was that mad about yesterday."

"Did you tell him?" demanded Michael Karl.

"No, sir. What would I be a-doin' that fer? He saw ye."

Michael Karl glanced nervously at the house, and, as he had expected ever since Evans had spoken, the stiff, ramrod figure of the Colonel stepped out on the terrace.

"You will please dismount and come in at once," said the Colonel dryly.

Feeling like a badly whipped small boy Michael Karl obeyed. The Colonel *would* wait until he was almost out of reach before he'd spring. As he had a hundred times before, Michael Karl rebelled silently against the Colonel's favorite cat and mouse game.

"I'll be a-tellin' the boy on the hill that ye're not comin'?" Evans whispered.

Michael Karl nodded and thanked him with a smile. He went in slowly to find the Colonel waiting in the hall.

"The library, please," said that gentleman crisply.

Once there the Colonel seated himself in the

desk chair while Michael Karl took his place before the desk. He had stood there so often he was surprised that the rug didn't show the wear. The Colonel let him stand awhile in silence before he began; that too was the usual procedure.

"You intend to become a soldier?"

"Yes," answered Michael Karl dutifully. He knew all the questions and answers by heart now.

"How do you expect to command men when you can't obey orders yourself?"

There was no answer for this one.

"Haven't you had distinct orders that you are not to speak to any one outside the gates unless it is absolutely necessary?"

"Yes, sir."

"Then why did you deliberately meet that young man on the hill yesterday and hold a long conversation with him?"

"Because," answered Michael Karl defiantly, "I wanted to."

The Colonel's sharp face showed no change though it was an unheard-of thing for Michael Karl to answer back.

"You keep me in here like some sort of a prisoner—I can't do this and I can't do that. And if I ride out I must take a groom to see that I don't speak with any one. Why?

"That fellow I spoke to yesterday was a scout-master out with his troop. I was interested and stopped to ask some questions. Was that a crime? Tell me, why do I have to live like this? Yesterday morning I didn't think this life was very strange; you always told me that wealthy boys had to live like this. But I learned some things from that scoutmaster and now I know that all wealthy boys aren't prisoners like I am. And why don't you ever mention my parents or answer my questions about them? Who and what am I?'' Michael Karl flung his questions at the stiff man behind the desk.

"Attention!'' snapped the Colonel, but for the first time in his life Michael Karl refused to obey.

"I'm through,'' he said flatly. "Unless you can give me some good reason why I should, I am through obeying orders. And now I'm going to take that ride you interrupted. And I'm going to the scout camp and stay as long as it pleases me.'' Michael Karl felt his power of rebellion growing with every word.

"You are going to your quarters under close arrest,'' said the Colonel quietly.

Close arrest meant his bedroom and bread and water for a week, but the threat failed to bring him to terms as it had in the past. Michael Karl was through with being a "bit of a coward.''

"And if I refuse?''

The Colonel lifted his eyebrows. "I hardly think that at your age you would desire being carried upstairs by the servants.''

Michael Karl flushed painfully. The Colonel was capable of ordering that very humiliating thing.

"You win,'' conceded Michael Karl. "But—''

"Yes?''

"Oh, what does it matter?'' Michael Karl was beaten again. He dragged up the stairs and into his room, hating himself.

It was a cheerless place, his room; the Colonel didn't believe in too much comfort. A cot bed, two straight-backed chairs, shelf of heavy, dull-looking books, a table and a lamp couldn't make the room look overcrowded. Michael Karl threw his gloves and crop on the table and went to stare out of the window before he thought of something and smiled.

The Colonel hadn't won on all points after all. Michael Karl pulled two of the solid books and felt behind them. Yes, it was still there.

He took out a blue book with limp covers. On one of his carefully supervised trips to town he had caught a glimpse of it in a window, and Evans had been sent to purchase it the next day. Before its purchase Kipling had been just a name in a literature book, and the Colonel went very light on literature as a part of Michael Karl's education. But now Kipling was a very real person who wrote gorgeous verse about soldiers.

Michael Karl curled up on the cot in a way that he knew the Colonel would hate and opened the book to the "Road to Mandalay," which he was learning. Let the Colonel think he was reading "Field Fortifications" or some such rot.

It wasn't the first time he had spent his hours in disgrace reading forbidden literature. Evans smuggled him the magazines, newspapers and books upon which the Colonel thought it unnecessary for him to waste his time. What Michael Karl knew about the America outside his gates, and it was a surprising lot, he had learned through reading.

The light had begun to fade when some one knocked on the door. Michael Karl crossed the room with guilty haste and slid the book back in its old hiding place.

"Who's there?" he asked.

"The Colonel wants to see you in the library, sir."

Michael Karl was startled. It wasn't like the Colonel to jaw him twice the same day. Unless, Michael Karl frowned, unless he had found that pile of magazines in the summer house.

With a guilty conscience as regards the magazines, he pulled his tie straight and smoothed down his hair. The Colonel worshiped neatness, and if Michael Karl went in to him with ruffled hair— The Colonel also insisted upon promptness, and Michael Karl clattered down the stairs at top speed.

Outside the library door he hesitated. The Colonel wasn't alone. Some one with a deep and growly voice was doing all the talking. Michael Karl had the queerest feeling of fear, as if he should not knock on that door but run as far from it as possible. He knew that there was something behind it which threatened him.

Michael Karl knocked.

"Come in," ordered the Colonel, and Michael Karl obeyed.

To his surprise the room seemed crowded with people and it took him a second or two to get them sorted out. What was even more disconcerting, he seemed to have released a spring when he opened the door, for they all clicked their heels and bent stiffly at the hips in his general direction.

"This is His Royal Highness," the Colonel was saying. Michael Karl felt as he once had when he missed a step at the head of the stairs and bumped down jerkily step by step.

Was he a Royal Highness? If so, why?

He appeared to be one all right. They, the fat red-faced man with the too-tight collar, the mummy in black, and the very pale young man, were all looking respectfully right at him, Michael Karl.

"A chair for His Royal Highness," commanded the fat man in the deep voice Michael Karl had heard through the door.

The pale young man dragged one out, and Michael Karl seated himself rather gingerly. This Highness business was decidedly upsetting. However, the Colonel looked as if he had eaten something sour, and that brightened things up a bit.

"His Royal Highness," said the Colonel in a thin, dry voice, "has been kept in ignorance of his rank in accordance with His late Majesty's wishes."

Michael Karl wished that they would quit talking about him in the third person, it made him feel as if he weren't there at all.

"Quite right, quite right," boomed the fat man. "You may inform His Royal Highness now."

The Colonel turned towards Michael Karl and began reciting in the monotonous tones of a lecturer. "Your Royal Highness's father was the second son of His Majesty, King Karl of Morvania. While an exile in America, he contracted a marriage which was highly displeasing to His Majesty. Prince Eric was killed with his bride in an accident soon after Your Royal Highness's birth. His Majesty gave orders that you should be educated as one of your rank but that you were not to enter Morvania unless you were sent for."

Michael Karl had been told all his life that a gentleman never shows emotion, but he couldn't control the little gasp of surprise. He, Michael Karl, was a prince, the grandson of a king. Now he knew it was a dream, one of those queer nightmares where everything is topsy-turvy.

"A year ago," the Colonel continued, "His Majesty was assassinated while visiting his city of Innesberg. And then the Council of Nobles assembled and took control of the government for one year in accordance with the law. Unfortunately the Crown Prince was killed in a mountain accident, and, the year of regency being ended, the throne passes to Your Royal Highness."

He stopped and they all stared at Michael Karl. Evidently he was expected to make some sort of an answer. What if he told them the truth? Michael Karl had no desire for royal honors. He had had more than a taste of a prince's life, if, as according to the Colonel, he had been living the life of one of his rank. All he wanted was his freedom.

He drew a deep breath.

"Nothing doing," said Michael Karl distinctly.

They all leaned forward as if they hadn't heard.

"May—may I ask what Your Royal Highness means by that extraordinary statement?" questioned the fat man at last.

"Just what I said. I'm through. You can go hunt up another king for your country. I'm an American citizen (he was basing his statement on something he had once read and hazily remembered) and I'm staying right here."

The Colonel broke the shocked silence. "With persons of Your Royal Highness's rank there is no question of citizenship. Your Royal Highness is sailing to-morrow."

His Royal Highness so far forgot himself as to murmur "Really?" at this observation.

"And just how are you going to get me out of the country if I don't want to go?"

"There are ways," answered the Colonel.

Michael Karl shivered. He knew something of the Colonel's "ways." Perhaps it would be better if he were to give in now and do his fighting later when they had forgotten to watch him. He had no idea where Morvania was, but it sounded like something in the Balkans and that was pretty far away. If he couldn't get away before they reached there, why, he'd deserve to be a prince.

"Perhaps," suggested the fat man suavely, "you had better present us to His Royal Highness."

The Colonel came to life again. "General Oberdamnn," the fat man clicked and bowed. Michael Karl immediately gained a very poor idea of the army which called him General. "Count Kafner," the mummy in black permitted itself a creaking bow. "And Baron von Urdlemann, Your Royal Highness's aide-de-camp," the pale young man bent forward. Michael Karl wondered if all Morvanians had that distressing shade of taffy-colored hair.

Michael Karl arose. He was puzzled about the editorial "we." Did princes use it or not? He decided against it.

"I thank you, gentlemen, for your attendance, and I trust we shall have a very pleasant journey." He seemed to have said the right thing; anyway, no one looked disturbed.

"Your Royal Highness desires to change? We leave in an hour," reminded General Oberdamnn glancing at Michael Karl's riding breeches and brown silk shirt.

So Michael Karl found himself being politely given his marching orders and out in the hall. The General, he guessed, was great on discipline, but he could be outwitted, thought Michael Karl as he climbed the stairs. Just now the mummy was the unknown quantity, but the aide-de-camp ought to be easy to handle.

The step behind him creaked, and Michael Karl glanced over his shoulder. Baron von Urdlemann was at his heels. It was Michael Karl's first taste of the goldfish life he was to enjoy for the next month.

Michael Karl changed his clothes and hung his breeches away in the closet with a sigh of regret. After all, he had had some fun. The Duchess had given him an afternoon or two worth while, like the time she had joined the fox hunt unbidden the fall of the year before.

The silent Baron stood by the door. Michael Karl had refused to allow him to act as valet. He didn't foresee the coming of dress uniforms when it would take both a valet and an aide-de-camp to get him properly stowed away behind the gold lace.

His bag stood ready packed by the door; already the room had lost all trace of his occupancy. No, there was one thing that wasn't gone. Michael Karl slipped into a trench coat whose patch pockets were oversize, and into one of them he stuffed his beloved Kipling book.

After a last look around he went out into the hall and down the stairs, with the Baron always the regulation two steps behind him. The General and the Count were both struggling into overcoats, and they seemed to be having some sort of an argument with the Colonel.

"My friend, I tell you again that there were no orders for you to accompany us, and without orders you may not."

Michael Karl felt that *that* announcement deserved some sort of recognition in the form of a cheer. Without the Colonel the expedition began to appear somewhat like a pleasant vacation. He even felt friendly towards the General.

So with no tears or other conventional signs of grief Michael Karl bade good-by to his guardian and climbed into the waiting car. He wasn't going to worry about the future, he decided, and immediately began wondering where Morvania was and how long it would be before he could slip away.

He was squeezed between the fat General and the thin Count on the back seat of the car while his silent aide-de-camp perched precariously on the tiny seat before them. They swept down the drive and out between the gates. The only thing Michael Karl regretted leaving was the Duchess, and he promised himself that he would come back and get her as soon as he was free.

As they rounded the slope of the hill the driver, being extra cautious (probably because of his precious freight, thought Michael Karl), slowed down. A small crowd of khaki-clothed boys were busy with red and white flags, signaling, Michael Karl guessed. He wished that he could get out and astonish the scoutmaster with his news. But the car swept on.

"These Boy Scouts, they are everywhere," observed the General.

"Your Royal Highness is the Commander-in-chief of the Morvanian Boy Scouts," his aide-de-camp informed him, and was frowned upon by the General who was just about to say the same thing.

Michael Karl couldn't think of anything to say except, "How interesting," which seemed rather flat.

Then a certain curiosity prompted him to ask, "What else am I?"

"Your Royal Highness is the Colonel of the Prince's Own, of the Red Hussars, of the Mounted Rifles, Commander-in-chief of the Air Force, Military Governor of Rein, Commander of the Fortress of St. Sebastian, Grand Master of the Order of St. Sebastian, Companion of the Order of the Crown, Hereditary Knight of the Palace, Champion of the King, Wearer of the Sword of St. Michael, Duke of Casonva, Baron of Urnt, Count of Kelive, Knight of Klam—"

"All that," murmured Michael Karl, slightly dazed.

"There is more, Your Royal Highness," said the General, eager to continue.

"That will be enough," said Michael Karl, firmly.

Chapter II

The Border and — Morvania

"If it snows," warned His Royal Highness, Crown Prince Michael Karl of Morvania, in a firm voice, "I shall probably yell," he considered this statement a moment and then added, "loudly."

His aide-de-camp murmured politely. Michael Karl took no notice of him, for he had become used to taking no notice of his everpresent aide-de-camp, a nice but exceedingly dull young man.

"Yes," Michael Karl continued, "I shall yell if I have to conceal this," with a sweep of his hand he indicated the splendor of the gold-laced sable tunic and well-cut riding breeches which happened to be adorning his royal person, "with that!" His Royal Highness pushed away a long cloak with a gesture of loathing. He had longed for a good American overcoat for days; these cloaks were very apt to trip the uninitiated wearer if he weren't careful.

Michael Karl leaned his forehead against the cool window pane of the Royal coach trying to see if the threatened snow was yet in sight. He was an unwilling inmate of the Royal Train bound for

Morvania, and he had not yet escaped.

For one thing he had never been alone long enough even to leave a room, the aide-de-camp had seen to that. Princes, Michael Karl had discovered, had just about as much private life as an alligator on exhibition in an animal store window. And every mile that he drew nearer to the border of his kingdom his chances lessened. Short of sand-bagging his attendant and committing suicide by leaping out of the train, which seemed to spend all its time wandering around on the edge of the most appalling cliffs, he didn't see how he was going to ever get free.

"How long is this going to last?" he demanded suddenly.

Baron von Urdlemann came to attention correctly, an annoying habit of his which would never allow Michael Karl to forget that he, Michael Karl, was a prince, and answered:

"We will reach Your Royal Highness's capital of Rein before midnight. The halfway station is a two hours' journey from here."

"The halfway station?"

"The train is forced to add another engine before it ascends the long pass, Your Royal Highness. We shall stop there about ten minutes, and the escort train will be there to greet us. A company of Your Royal Highness's own regiment has been given that honor."

"Oh!" said Michael Karl blankly. A company of his own regiment, that meant speeches and things. He shuddered slightly. Would he ever forget what had happened at the Morvanian embassy in Paris when he had been bullied into making a speech?

And Berlin, but he preferred not to think about what had happened in Berlin.

London had been easier. Michael Karl sighed; he had always wanted to see London, but now all he could remember of it was a suite of rather dingy hotel rooms and a long thin man who came to whisper with Count Kafner.

He leaned back in the red velvet-covered seat, and his elbow came into sharp contact with something he had carefully tucked behind him at Count Kafner's last entrance. The Count had turned out to be a snooper of the worst sort, and Michael Karl didn't trust him even when he could see him.

Michael Karl glanced cautiously at the Baron, but that gentleman had apparently sunk back into the solemn day-dream which occupied him whenever his royal master didn't require his attention. From behind him Michael Karl drew out the Kipling book which had shared all his amazing adventures.

The publishers had been exceedingly generous with this volume. There were four blank pages in the front and eight at the back, all of which Michael Karl was using to a very good advantage. With pen or pencil, whichever he could find at the moment, he was putting down all he could learn, or overhear, or think about this country of his and the people in it. Neither the Count nor the General would have been flattered at their pen portraits in Michael Karl's book.

Michael Karl found the pencil he had secreted in the top of his trim boot and thoughtfully made an entry concerning the halfway station. One never could tell when such information might become useful.

A sentence concerning the General's table manners caught his eye and he chuckled. Some one rapped on the compartment door, and he thrust the book out of sight guiltily. The aide-de-camp jumped to open the door. He always moved with the wooden exactness of well-oiled machinery.

Count Kafner rustled in, and Michael Karl sighed wearily. Of all his enforced companions, he liked the Count the least. The man was just like a mummy out of a museum.

"Your Royal Highness," began the Count with a heel-clicking bow. His long yellow fingers were fiddling with a purple velvet jewel case.

"Your Royal Highness," he began again, rather dashed at the coolness of his reception. Evidently His Royal Highness was supposed to play up to him.

"Yes?" Michael Karl encouraged him none too heartily.

"These," Count Kafner held the jewel case one inch nearer. "Your Royal Highness should assume these now. It will be necessary to wear them when appearing before the officers who will greet Your Royal Highness at the halfway station."

He snapped open the case and held out for Michael Karl's somewhat awed inspection the two most wonderful jewels he had ever seen. A crown of gold studded with rubies lay on a bed of scarlet ribbon while above it on the black satin lining of the case rested a cross formed by two broad silver arrows set in diamonds which, in the light, sparkled and flashed like one great stone.

The Count handed the case to the Baron and lifted out the crown with his dry unpleasant fingers.

"If Your Royal Highness will arise and allow me to adjust it," he suggested.

Michael Karl stumbled to his feet. He was supposed to wear those—those wonders!

"This is the Order of the Crown, Your Royal Highness. The ribbon goes across the shoulder—so." The Count pulled the scarlet ribbon over Michael Karl's right shoulder and fastened it in some mysterious way under his left arm so that the crown shone with magnificent dullness from the tangled gold cords which crossed the breast of his black tunic.

"And this, Your Royal Highness, is the Grand Cross of the Order of St. Sebastian. If I may slip this over Your Royal Highness's head—" Michael Karl bent his head and the cross slid down to join the crown.

The Count took the empty case from the Baron and bowed stiffly.

"I thank Your Royal Highness," he rasped in his dry voice and bowed himself back into the corridor. Michael Karl shrank back into his seat. Thinking of the thousands of dollars which must be hanging about him now, he shivered slightly. He was not a coward, but a gunman, right now, was the last thing he would like to meet.

"Are there any bandits in Morvania?" he asked even before he thought.

The Baron started and looked at Michael Karl queerly.

"There is one," he said slowly. "He has his head-quarters somewhere in these mountains."

"Who is he?"

"They call him Black Stefan but the peasants have an uglier name for him—Werewolf. He is supposed to be a man by day and a wolf by night and his followers are reported to have been recruited from the graveyards."

"Pleasant."

"Yes. He is the only bandit who has successfully defied the government. Why, just last month he raided a government outpost in the mountains. The peasants report that he hates the government bitterly, has some sort of grudge against all Morvanians of the ruling class. We have never been able to find his headquarters, he is too well served. No peasant or mountaineer would betray the Werewolf."

"D'you know, Baron, I'm beginning to enjoy this trip. Any chance of our meeting this Werewolf?"

For the first time since Michael Karl had met him the Baron showed emotion. "I hope not, Your Royal Highness!"

"Then you believe there is some chance?" demanded Michael Karl, his eyes alight.

"The halfway station is the danger point, Your Royal Highness. If the escort train should be delayed—"

"Let's hope that it will be," said Michael Karl surprisingly.

Baron von Urdlemann stared at him uncertainly. Michael Karl had a queer sense of humor, but then again he might really have meant that mad wish. Puzzled, the aide-de-camp made no answer. This American Prince often bewildered him.

Meanwhile Michael Karl was staring out at the distant snow-capped mountains. So there was a Werewolf bandit "in them thar hills," one who successfully defied the government and hated the nobles. Probably a sort of up-to-date Robin Hood. On any count Black Stefan was a chap worth meeting. Michael Karl wished with all his might that the Werewolf would have the audacity to hold up the Royal Train. That would be worth being dragged to Morvania for.

And how the Count and the General would enjoy it! If they, and some of the odd specimens he had seen in the embassies, were representatives of the ruling class, no wonder Stefan had no time for it. Michael Karl would gladly pay him to rid the country of them.

A flake of snow struck the window to be followed by another and another. Michael Karl wondered idly what his stiff aide-de-camp would do if he carried out his threat and yelled. But the game wasn't really worth the effort. He felt for his book and scribbled in the presentation of the orders and thought that if they hung much more on him he would look like a Christmas tree.

The train slowed down, and Baron von Urdle-mann with a murmured apology went to look out of the other window. Some one knocked, and the General edged his bulging uniform through the narrow door.

"The escort train is late. It will be best if Your Royal Highness remain in the compartment," he puffed.

Michael Karl nodded curtly and the General wriggled out again. So the escort train was late? Well, here was Black Stefan's chance to bag one perfectly good Crown Prince and some assorted cabinet members, to say nothing of the Royal Train itself. Too bad the poor chap didn't know about it.

Baron von Urdlemann was edging about restlessly. At last he ventured to offend against etiquette and address Michael Karl without being spoken to.

"I don't like it, Your Royal Highness," he said nervously. "The escort had very strict orders."

"You think that this Black Stefan may be going to amuse himself?" asked Michael Karl eagerly.

But the Baron wouldn't answer directly. He made some lagging reply and went over by the door, but Michael Karl caught a glimpse of a revolver. So the Baron did think just that.

Michael Karl made up his mind that here was going to be no "defend the Prince to the death" stuff. He'd knock out the Baron himself first. After all, life as a bandit's prisoner had more appeal than life as the Crown Prince of Morvania and the worst thing the Werewolf could do was to send him on into the arms of his loving subjects, or so Michael Karl thought. He changed his ideas considerably, later that evening.

But if the Prince was going to be a prisoner, and somehow Michael Karl knew he was going to be, that was no reason why the royal jewels should fall into the unwashed hands of some border ruffian. They belonged to no private individual but to the state.

He carefully unfastened the ribbon of the crown and let the whole thing slide into his hand. Where could it be put that a none too careful searcher would miss it?

High on the wall was the ventilator which led to the neighboring compartment. Michael Karl stepped onto the seat and found that by stretching he could just reach the edge. He let the Crown slide into the opening and fastened the ribbon to a hook which had once held a screen across the mouth. If the bandits didn't have much time for a search, the Crown was safe.

"Why are you doing that, Your Royal Highness?"

"Just playing safe, Baron. The jewels are my responsibility and—" Michael Karl allowed his explanation to trail off when he saw that the Baron understood.

He groped for the Cross among the gold cords but before he could slip the chain over his head the train stopped. There was no chance to find a hiding place for it now; he'd have to slip it inside his shirt and trust to luck. Michael Karl unhooked the high collar of his tunic and dropped the Cross inside. When its icy smoothness touched his bare throat it made him jump. Here was hoping that the bandits wouldn't search prisoners too closely.

What a thump he'd look if no bandit turned up. It would be just his luck. They sat uneasily in the royal compartment while the traveling clock above the Baron's head ticked off five minutes; it took ten minutes to add the engine. Black Stefan had five minutes' grace.

A muffled voice from the corridor startled them

both. The Baron opened the door and conferred with the visitor in an undertone. Michael Karl caught the words "General" and "First Compartment"; evidently the Baron was wanted up front.

"Your Royal Highness, General Oberdamnn desires my attendance at once. It would be better if Your Royal Highness were to remain here," he said and, hesitating before he hurried away frowning, he added, "This is most unusual. My orders were not to leave Your Royal Highness alone."

"Go ahead," urged Michael Karl.

He paced nervously up and down, two minutes, three. He might as well give up, Black Stefan hadn't snapped at the bait. Perhaps he thought there was some sort of a catch in it. What a country. Not one of its inhabitants had any ambition or drive, not even the gunmen.

Turning, he snatched up the hated cloak. At least he could get some fresh air on the platform at the end. The Kipling book caught his eye as he was going out and he took it with him. If he left it, that snooping Count would be sure to find it.

The platform door was locked but a door leading out onto the track itself was invitingly open. There was no danger in going out, Michael Karl thought bitterly; even Black Stefan had failed him.

The gravel between the rails scraped his shining boots, and the falling snow caught in the fur collar of his cloak and in his uncovered hair. He shivered in the cold damp wind blowing down from the mountains and turned to step back into the train. But Michael Karl was never to enter the Royal Train.

From close by in the forest came an eerie cry

followed by a yapping chorus, and out of the trees at the edge of the gravel swept a little band of dark horses attended by a howling pack of what Michael Karl first thought were dogs. And then he saw more clearly—they were wolves!

The riders were an uncanny mixture of wolf and man, masked completely by shaggy gray wolf skins drawn over the upper parts of their bodies. They cantered silently down upon the train in dead quiet except for the excited yelps of their four-footed companions whom they kept in order with long whips.

Black Stefan had come! The wolfmen spread out in a thin line. They did not seem to expect resistance, for the very good reason, as Michael Karl discovered later, that a confederate on the train had neatly disposed of guns and all other things which might mean trouble for them. He had even drawn the Baron away from the Royal Compartment with a faked message.

There were shouts from the engine now; the wolfmen had been discovered. Michael Karl stood like a spectator at a play watching it all as four-footed and two-footed wolves faded into the blackness by the engines.

He stepped farther out to see the better. There was an unpleasant growl, and Michael Karl's arms were seized from behind in a steely grip.

"Will you come quietly?" inquired his unknown captor, surprisingly in English, "or—?"

The "or" was accompanied by a sharp prick between his shoulders.

Michael Karl suddenly felt his temper slipping. This was what he had wanted, and yet he had an almost ungovernable desire to choke this fellow behind him if he could. He was pricked again very suggestively.

"I'll come quietly," he answered in English and then hastened to repeat his answer in the few words of halting Morvanian he had learned from Baron von Urdlemann during the past month.

His captor laughed unpleasantly. "I thought you would," he said scornfully. "None of you baby officers have an ounce of pluck. Down, Dark One," he admonished something which was sniffing at Michael Karl's boots. "This one isn't your meat—yet."

A wolfman came up leading three horses and Michael Karl was roughly urged to mount. His wrists had been tied behind him. From by the engine the pack, both four-footed and two-footed, came drifting back.

"Did you find him?" demanded the man who had captured Michael Karl.

Some one mumbled an answer in the negative. There were no other prisoners, and for the first time Michael Karl began to be afraid. As if he had read Michael Karl's thoughts the man beside him grunted through his wolf mask:

"Your friends are all right, little one. We just tied them up and left them for the other train crew to find when they get that brace of logs we left for them off the track and are able to steam down. We're taking you to the Chief. He feeds little things like you to the wolves when he's angry, so you better keep a straight tongue in your head, youngster."

Michael Karl held on to his temper. After all, in

a way he had asked for this. And he knew a trick that Evans, his old groom, had taught him so that when the time came he could go Houdini one better.

They followed some sort of a faint trail up the mountain side. It was quite dark now and the leader, producing a torch, set it alight. This, Michael Karl supposed, was what the writing chaps called an adventure. He would be more interested if he wasn't so cold. This affair would be a lesson to him always to bring a cap along when he went walking in the evening. The Kipling book, which he had wedged into an inner pocket in the cloak, was making itself unpleasant by banging against his ribs. He tried to cheer himself by the thought that he was free from speeches at last, and then he remembered gloomily what the wolfman had said concerning his tongue. Evidently he was slated to talk before the mysterious chief himself.

The four-footed captors were beginning to pay him attentions which he didn't altogether relish. They seemed to think it great fun to jump at his feet or steal up behind and make his horse shy by growling. At first the wolfmen laughed, and then when Michael Karl's horse caused them too much trouble they uncoiled their black whips and snapped them viciously at the narrow gray muzzles.

The wolves seemed to fear the whips, and at the sight of one would slink away. Michael Karl filed that fact away for future use.

They were still going up, but now they took a path along the mountain side so narrow that

Michael Karl's one boot scraped along the wall while the other seemed to dangle out over the edge of a cliff. Michael Karl decided that he did not like the mountains.

The trail wound around a rock and Michael Karl caught a glimpse of a light in the valley below. It seemed to interest the wolfmen.

"The Crown Inn," one of them pointed to the distant light.

Another spat over the cliff in contempt. "The landlord's jelly. He'd run with the hare and hunt with the hounds if he had the courage, but he hasn't, so he just sits there and shakes when he hears the hunting horn. He's a fool and a coward. We'll burn him out some night and good riddance."

"I hear," said some one behind Michael Karl with a smack of his lips, "that a rich American is staying there. Wants to do some mountain climbing. All Americans are mad."

"You will leave him alone, you. We are not to get mixed up with foreigners, it causes too much unpleasantness. Those are orders."

"But," protested the rebuked one unhappily, "Americans are so rich."

"They also have Consuls," said the leader significantly.

Michael Karl stared down at the light as long as he could see it. If he could reach that American—

"Here we are, little one," said his captor, and they clattered over a bridge into a stone-paved courtyard.

Chapter III

A Prince Meets A Werewolf

Black Stefan's stronghold must have once been a great lord's castle, dominating and levying tribute upon the long valley at its foot. Now when the keep, inner and outer walls, in fact all but the lord's tower lay in ruins, it still had the power to overawe the newcomer.

Michael Karl was pulled down from his horse and stood, shivering more with excitement and cold than with fear, in the light of great pine torches thrust through iron rings on the walls. The wolves were prowling about, sniffing at the prisoner and at a great two-wheeled cart loaded with farm produce which had groaned in over the moat bridge.

There seemed to be no concealment, no hush-hush. Evidently what Baron von Urdlemann had said was true, no one dared to betray Black Stefan to the soldiers.

His captor hurried him across the courtyard through a heavy door and into a long hall whose only furnishing seemed to be an oversized table pushed to one side. Michael Karl had a sudden vision of the wolf pack, two-footed and four-footed, growling around a loaded board while the mysterious Werewolf brooded at the head of his table.

But a moment later, when the fire on the mammoth hearth flickered, he saw a dais at the head of the table two steps high and occupied by a single high-backed chair. It stood, draped with a crimson cloak, like a throne—a bandit's throne. Black Stefan must hold almost royal state. Who was he really?

Michael Karl was hurried across to the hearth and there motioned to seat himself on a bench. Apparently the Werewolf wasn't ready to see him. The wolfman, after tying his feet to one of the bench legs, left him and hurried out.

"Going to report," decided Michael Karl.

The American at the Crown Inn interested him. Such a man, "mad as all Americans," according to the wolfman, might be reckless enough to help him if he could once escape the wolfmen.

He stopped thinking about the American and tried to shrug his heavy cloak farther back on his shoulders. The fire was altogether too warm. Burying his chin in the fur collar he tugged at the hooks, but, unfortunately, they held. It looked as if he must play his best card or roast to death. After all, the wolfman might believe that he had tied his prisoner too loosely.

Rolling his thumb across his palm until his hand was hardly any larger than his wrist, he discovered that for once his small hands served him well. He started to free his hands, working by eighths of inches and losing more than a little skin in the process. With a last smarting tug the cords slipped off and he was free.

Michael Karl rubbed his burning wrists and then hastened to unhook his collar and throw aside his cloak before unfastening his feet. As he leaned forward he felt the Cross slide across his breast. Here was hoping that he would not be searched. Should he proclaim his rank or should he pretend to be only an aide-de-camp? Any way around he would get an unpleasant greeting if the Werewolf hated the nobles as the Baron had said he did.

The Crown Inn down the valley, with its American guest, was worth attempting. Catching up his discarded cloak he looked around the empty hall. Why not now?

"I trust you are not leaving us?"

Michael Karl turned slowly. On the dais stood a tall man, wolf-masked like all the rest he had seen, but, somehow different. The newcomer wore authority like a cloak; he was no common member of the pack for all his rough pelt and shaggy mask.

Thre were whisperings and murmuring behind them, the wolf pack was filing in to join the fun.

"Enter the villain," announced Michael Karl clearly, still impressed by the melodrama of it all. Really it was too much like a certain movie he had once disobediently attended.

"Just so," agreed the masked newcomer, "only I am afraid that we might differ upon the identity of the villain. Now you, of course, have cast me for that role, while I have quite definitely selected you for the part."

"Of course, that is to be expected," answered

Michael Karl politely. "But then the audience," he glanced around at the assembled pack, "are prepared to agree with you." He wondered desperately just how long they would keep this sort of thing up.

"You are Black Stefan?" he inquired.

The masked leader nodded curtly.

"And you?" Black Stefan's voice had a stern "come to business" like note in it now.

Michael Karl wished he could see his enemy's face; fighting from behind a mask wasn't sporting: perhaps if things got too hot he would mention that fact.

"I shall leave that answer to you. After all you can't expect me to be too helpful."

He fingered his cloak and measured the distance between him and the door. If he could keep this fellow talking he might have a very slim chance. Michael Karl no longer believed that the perfect life was to be found as a prisoner of the Werewolf. "Boys of your age," commented the Werewolf, "do not usually wear the uniforms of Colonels, especially the uniform of the Commander of the Prince's Own." Michael Karl made no answer, recognizing the Werewolf's cat and mouse game. The bandit knew who he was all right, he was just amusing himself by pretending he didn't.

"Search him," the Werewolf commanded suddenly.

His cloak was snatched from his hands and his tunic literally torn from his shoulders. They were rougher than they need be, he thought, as his shirt ripped under their clumsy hands until he was afraid it would follow his tunic.

An unwilling button snapped off, and the white silk pulled open on his breast, allowing the diamond cross with its icy fire to dangle through. At the sight of it they drew back, and the Werewolf leaned forward with a little cry.

"So," he said quietly, "we are honored in entertaining His Royal Highness, the Crown Prince?"

"Yes," said Michael Karl simply.

The man on the dais bowed mockingly. "Forgive us for not receiving you with the honor due Your Royal Highness, but it has been so long since one of your illustrious rank has paid us a visit. The last one," Black Stefan shook his head sadly, "the last one departed somewhat suddenly. You have perhaps heard of Ulrich Karl?"

Michael Karl caught his breath sharply. "The Crown Prince who was killed in the mountains."

"Just so. He was unfortunate. I have a feeling that all of your family will be unfortunate in the mountains, Your Royal Highness. The mountain air seems very unhealthy for one of your name."

"Then you killed him?" demanded Michael Karl. He had been told nothing about his cousin except that he had died in a mountain accident.

Black Stefan's mouth smiled under the wolf muzzle. It wasn't a nice smile. "Shall we say that he became displeasing to certain mountaineers who settle their own quarrels? There is bad blood in you, princeling."

"At least," Michael Karl faced him, "at least I am not a murderer."

"No? Then what, my Prince, of the men who have disappeared in your Lion Tower?"

Michael Karl was honestly bewildered. "I don't

know what you mean."

"Erich, tell what you know," ordered Black Stefan.

The wolfman who had captured Michael Karl mounted the lower step of the dais and turned to face them.

"There was in the bodyguard of the king a certain young man who dared to speak aloud what other men whispered. He disappeared into the Lion Tower two months ago, nor has he returned."

Through Erich's mask his eyes red with hate bored down upon Michael Karl. His broad hands were playing with a hunting knife.

"Not yet, my friend," purred Black Stefan. "And now, my Prince, what have you to say?"

"I am not responsible for what the late king did," said Michael Karl firmly. "I have not even been in Morvania before."

The green eyes of the Werewolf were burning straight into his. "Morvania has not changed since the feudal days," said the Werewolf. "The king is responsible to no one, but he is held responsible for the deeds of his ancestors. You are the last of the Karloffs, a mad, bad race. What is there to prevent me making an end to you and your horrors to-night? The country would worship me for it."

Michael Karl felt an icy curtain of terror slip down upon him. This man was mad. He would do just what he was proposing and smile at the deed. The Werewolf was waiting for something. Perhaps he wanted Michael Karl to beg for his life; well, that he would never do.

"If that is how you feel, well, I'm fairly helpless,

am I not? And you have a crew of assistant murderers, if you don't care to soil your own hands."

Some one caught his skinned wrists, and Erich openly drew his knife. Through all his fear Michael Karl had an insane desire to laugh. It was too impossible, they must be doing it for the movies. Things like this didn't happen in this year of grace even in the most feudal of Balkan states. He couldn't keep from laughing any longer.

Looking straight into the Werewolf's mask he demanded, "How much do you pay your extras a day?"

The Werewolf hesitated. "So you think this is a cinema?"

"Well, really, things like this don't happen nowadays."

Black Stefan smiled. "I will say this for your kind, they have courage. But a night in the West Room usually brings them to terms. Take him away," he ended swiftly.

They hurried him out of the farther door and up a flight of steps worn into deep hollows by the passing and repassing of hundreds of feet. The passage was bitter cold, and Michael Karl longed for his cloak and tunic. By some mystery the Cross still swung at his throat, and it appeared that he was to be allowed to keep it.

Halfway down the corridor at the top of the stairs they were halted by a messenger hurrying after them. He delivered an order in a Morvanian dialect unknown to Michael Karl, whose guards opened the nearest oaken door on the corridor and thrust him in. The American heard the key rasp in the lock and their heavy boots clamping on the stairs in an awful hurry to get somewhere.

The room he stood in was small and dark, furnished, he discovered by the simple method of walking around and bumping into things, with a shaky table, a rude cot and a three-legged stool. Higher than his head a window was a pale square on the wall.

He pushed the table against the wall, supporting its weak leg with the stool and clambered up carefully. A story below his window lay the courtyard and even as he watched, a group of wolfmen mounted and rode furiously out, leaving the yard empty except for wandering wolves, most of whom were waiting patiently by a small door at one end.

Their patience was at last rewarded by the coming of one of the wolfmen, who tossed them great chunks of meat and then stood by, armed with a whip, to keep them from fighting. The meat bolted, they went to curl up in a furry mass near the farther wall.

Michael Karl measured the window, and then went to grope over the cot. Blankets or covers there were none, but after pulling off a stiff hide he discovered to his joy that a woven net of leather strips supported the sleeper. The knots, old and stiff, defied his fingers.

After his fifth attempt to undo one he leaned back against the wall exhausted, only to have something sharp press into his neck. Three of the links of the chain which held the Cross had sharp edges. Michael Karl slipped the chain over his head and set to work to saw the rope below the knots.

Fortune smiled on him at last, for when the thong parted he discovered that he need only to cut one more knot to get the whole thing loose. Cold from the stone floor where he crouched and from the unpaned window above stiffened his hands so that time and time again the chain slipped through his blue fingers and he had to grope around for it in the floor dust.

Once the rope was free he tested as best he could every foot of it. It would be fatal if it were to break and let him down into the midst of the waiting wolves. The cot had served him once and now it must serve him again. He knotted one end of the rope about the leg.

With his stiff fingers he tugged and twisted his snug boots until he managed to slip them off and fasten them about his waist with a couple of turns of the loose end of the rope. Coiling the slack in one hand he climbed his table ladder and began to wriggle through the window. It was a scraping tight fit and for the second time that night he had reason to be thankful that he was slim and small. A man of the Baron's or the Werewolf's size could never have made it.

Gasping as the chill mountain air struck him, he edged through and swung over to dangle against the rough masonry. Inch by inch he gingerly lowered himself, keeping watch on the sleeping wolves.

"If," he thought, "I ever get out of this, you'll never find me two blocks from Broadway again." He knew nothing of Broadway, but judging by the Balkans, it must be very safe. Michael Karl was through with adventure, but unfortunately, it wasn't through with him.

The rope didn't quite reach, of course, and he had to hang there, unfasten himself and his boots and then drop about four feet. The plump of his landing sounded alarmingly loud and without looking to see its effect on the sleeping guardians, he stumbled as fast as he could to the door of what he had identified earlier in the evening as the stable. Once in he slid the door to behind him with a sigh of relief.

A lantern was burning dimly at the far end and in its feeble light he sat down on a bale of hay and induced his numb feet to enter the boots, pulling at the black leather tops until they unrolled and fit snugly up around his thighs. They had been made high for campaign wear, fording rivers and so forth.

A row of saddles hung across a rack directly below the lantern. Thanking fate that he had learned to saddle a horse, Michael Karl snatched the nearest one and the blanket which hung behind it.

There were four horses left in the stalls, a rangy gray with a wicked eye, two roans and a black mare. Michael Karl longed for the Duchess who knew how to show her heels upon the occasion. He chose the gray and saddled and bridled him.

In the back of the gray's stall he came upon a find, a peasant's black overblouse, to take the place of his lost tunic. Pulling it over his head he led the gray toward the stable door. He could hear an alarming sniffing from the outside. The wolf pack was awake at last.

He was debating whether to take a chance and

attempt to ride them down or whether to hunt another exit when he caught a glimpse of one of the long whips, which all the wolfmen carried, hanging by the door. From what he had seen, he knew that the wolves feared the very sight of those whips. Michael Karl pulled it down and fastened its handle thong around his skinned wrist.

Mounting the gray, who was inclined to resent his actions, he pushed aside the sliding door with one hand and was out among the wolves. One crouched and sprang with a growl but Michael Karl swung the whip so that its tip stung the beast, and he fell back into the pack, which drew off sullenly, allowing the gray and his rider into the courtyard.

Michael Karl snapped the whip twice again and then used his spurs. The gray leapt like a hunted thing, trying to get away from the raking spurs of his rider by springing forward and they were out of the courtyard, drumming over a blurred moat bridge and into the forest before Michael Karl realized that he was really free.

Not daring to turn aside for fear of getting lost, he followed the trail downwards in record time. And without warning he dashed headlong upon what he had most wanted to avoid, the wolfmen returning to the Castle.

In the darkness he was upon them and almost through their band before they realized that anything was wrong. Some one snatched at his bridle, but Michael Karl used the wolf whip to good advantage. He saw grasping hands and masked faces under a wavering torch light and then he was through and riding for his life down the valley road.

The gray had gone mad with terror and Michael Karl could no longer control him. What he feared was that they would turn the wolves loose to hunt him down. With a sudden swerve, the gray left the trail and fled into the forest. Michael Karl ducked, riding with his face buried in the gray's rough mane, to escape the low branches which swept his shoulders and once scratched him deeply on the cheek.

They were shooting at him now, though surely in the darkness they couldn't see him. The wolf-men must be aiming at the crashing he made in the bushes. If they were, they were better than good shots. More than one bullet sped by too close for comfort.

With a plunge which left him giddy the gray half-slid, half-leaped down the steep bank of a mountain rivulet and essayed to cross on the stony bottom of the icy stream. It was here they came to grief. The gray stumbled, and Michael Karl shot over his head to land face downward, half in, half out of the numbing water.

The gray threw up his head, regained his feet, and was away before the dazed Michael Karl could make more than a feeble grab at the dangling reins. There was just a chance that the pursuers might follow the riderless horse by the sound of its passing and allow Michael Karl to creep away unseen.

He struggled up the bank and into a tangle of budding willow trees just as the first of the wolfmen appeared on the opposite bank. With a cry the wolfman urged his unwilling horse down the bank and into the stream. He was not alone. Out of the trees behind came several dark riders bunched together. Michael Karl counted them as they splashed across the stream. There were eight.

As he had hoped, they took the trail of the gray, and as long as they didn't bring out the wolves to share the chase he was safe. He waited until all the noise of their passing died away and then crept out of his hiding place.

The last dash of the gray had completely bewildered him. He no longer knew in what direction the road lay or where the Crown Inn was. But all streams must run down the valley and he would be fairly safe in following the river before him.

The water gave him an idea. Somewhere he had read that running water carried away scent and that hunted animals sometimes took to wading along streams to save themselves from dogs. With the fear of the keen-scented wolf pack always in his mind Michael Karl stepped into the swift but shallow water and started down stream.

Far in the distance he could hear shots and cries. Evidently the gray was still aiding him nobly. The chill of the water penetrated his boots and crept up his legs making him long for the royal carriage he had left so blithely hours before.

But he was free. Free from all of them. The General and the Count would think the Werewolf had him, and the Werewolf would think that he was trying to make his way to his supporters in Rein. All he had to do was lie low and he would be free of both of them and, when he got a chance, could slip out of the country and work his way back to America.

There was the obstacle of no passport of course. But he'd find some way to get around that if he had to go to America as a Morvanian immigrant.

The squashiness of his boots began to alarm him, and he waded back to the shore only to discover that walking in water soaked boots is about the most uncomfortable job in the world. It certainly didn't pay to be a prince. Though in justice he would have to admit that he had brought this last adventure on himself.

He had begun to wonder whether this stream ever would lead him any place when he heard a crashing and the stamping of horses alarmingly near. Stepping behind a tree he strained his eyes trying to catch sight of the riders.

A wolfman rode into the clearing not twenty feet away, and directly behind Michael Karl a twig snapped. They were having a drag hunt for him.

Then he did the worst thing he could have done. He lost his head and took to his heels. With a shout the wolfman was after him. Michael Karl sped down the valley hampered by his soaked boots. He was sure that if he could reach the inn he would be safe.

Sobbing for air in his tortured lungs he broke into the open and stumbled on a road running in great ruts towards a light. He had discovered by chance the road to the inn. Riding easily behind him came the wolfmen. Fearing every minute that they would close in, he dared not even glance behind him but panted on.

Chapter IV

In And Out Of The Crown Inn

For some reason his pursuers were holding back, perhaps they were planning to dig him out like a fox gone to ground. Now and then when he was silhouetted against a melting snow-drift one of them would fire, but the shot, perhaps purposely, would go wild. He staggered on around a curve in the road and with a last effort dragged himself into the bushes at the side.

Michael Karl lay face down in the half frozen mud, panting, too tired to care when the wolfmen cantered easily by and left him outside their narrowing circle. The chill in the ground forced him up again and he stumbled on towards the light.

Just as he fell against the stone wall of the inn there was a sharp crack and a chip flaked off the stone beside his weary head. They had seen him again. Exerting every bit of his disappearing strength he pulled himself up and dived head first through an open casement window while a bullet buried itself in the wooden sill above his head.

For a moment he was content to lie with his

cheek pressed close to the dusty floor and try to count the many aches which were torturing him. His shoulder, which he had twisted when the gray had thrown him but which he had not felt before, thumped dully.

"Of course, I don't mind visitors," observed a cool voice, "but the usual entrance is through the door, is it not?"

Michael Karl raised himself on his elbow. A young man with laughing eyes and a gay mouth was smiling down at him, the mad American who was defying the Werewolf by climbing his mountains.

Before Michael Karl could answer there was a tinkle of glass and one of the window panes splintered. The American crossed the room in two strides and slammed a heavy shutter across the window.

"Don't tell me," he begged, "that this is a revolution?"

Michael Karl sat up gingerly. Finding that his blistered feet would still bear him without complaining too much, he crawled up with the aid of a chair.

"No," he said, "I hate to disappoint you, but it isn't a revolution, it's a bandit!"

"You're a bandit?" demanded the American eagerly.

Michael Karl shook his head again. "No, our friends with the pop guns. There are eight of them."

"But," protested the American, "they followed you right up there. Where are the police?"

"That," said Michael Karl wearily, "is just the

point. There are no police. I have been told that
the army and the Werewolf are at odds, but so far
he's got the best of it. He rules this part of the
country."

The American laughed delightedly. "So he's
real, this Werewolf?"

Michael Karl lowered himself into a chair with a
groan. "If he isn't," he answered, "I've been having some mighty bad dreams."

"But I thought that he just went for the nobility."

Michael Karl caught a glimpse of himself in the
mirror. His face was streaked with mud and blood
and the peasant's blouse, which smelt vilely of the
stable, was ripped on one shoulder. No wonder the
American didn't believe that he was of high rank.

"Though you may not believe it," replied
Michael Karl slowly, "you see before you a late,
very late, Captain of the Prince's Own and a
Knight of Morvania. Unfortunately I am near
enough a noble to interest the Werewolf."

"You are an American," his questioner stated
rather than asked.

"Yes," admitted Michael Karl. "And so was the
late Crown Prince. This," he added with some
heat, "is what comes of helping your friends.
Michael Karl of Morvania was summoned home to
rule over this forsaken country and, like a fool, I
agreed to come along as his aide-de-camp. If I ever
get out of here I shall never even go as far as
Atlantic City again. I want to go and settle down in
St. Louis and never see the ocean or hear of anything on this side of the water again."

"What's happened?" demanded the American.

"Everything! We stopped," continued Michael Karl, "at that confounded halfway station to add another engine, and that fool Michael Karl thought it would be fun to get out and walk. Fun— ye gods! The Werewolf was up and had us before we got off the car steps, and I've been spending the evening in his stronghold."

"What happened to the Prince?"

"The usual thing, treat him well and hold him for ransom, and I hope it's a good long time before it's paid. He got me into this mess and then he sits up there too scared to try and save himself by sliding down a rope. Well, there he is, and there can he stay until General Oberdamnn comes and gets him."

"What are you going to do?"

"Get out of Morvania as fast as I can leg it, after I do a little job in Rein." Michael Karl felt for the Cross beneath his shirt. He must deliver that to some on in power before he was free.

Something crashed against the door below. The Wolfmen were forcing an entrance. Michael Karl arose painfully to his feet and, catching sight of a dull gleam among the American's scattered papers on the table, lurched over to arm himself with a wicked looking revolver.

The American had tiptoed to the door and was listening.

"It looks," he informed Michael Karl, "as if we are going to have some fun."

Michael Karl twisted his sore face into a battered smile.

"It does, doesn't it?" he answered.

And then blackness settled down about him. He swayed and crumpled to the floor.

Then he was warm, warmer than he had been for a long time. Michael Karl opened his eyes. He was lying half buried in a feather bed while the American cut the water-soaked boots off his swollen feet. It was good just to lie and let the waves of warmness beat about his chilled body while some one else struggled with those punishing boots of his.

He sighed with pleasure and the American looked up.

"Feeling better?" he asked.

Michael Karl nodded and then frowned. There was something he must remember, something he must guard.

"There," the American tossed aside the last bedraggled strip of leather.

"I say, son, what have you been doing to your feet?"

"Walking," answered Michael Karl dreamily, "walking miles and miles—in the water," he added.

The American produced a roll of bandage, a couple of bottles and a basin of water.

"Carry a first-aid kit with me," he explained. "You never know what might turn up."

"Like a Cro—" began Michael Karl and then changed it hastily to "captain."

Then he suddenly remembered. "Did they come in?"

The American laughed and shook his head. "I just threatened them with Uncle Sam, and they backed out. They know better than to go fooling around with Americans."

Michael Karl was puzzled. He didn't believe that the Werewolf would let the Crown Prince go with such little effort to retain him.

"Now, how's that?" The last bandage was fastened.

"Much better. Though they feel like they need a vacation."

"They're going to get one. You can't walk on those for a couple of days, young man. I wonder if these will fit." He produced a pair of pajamas amazingly long in sleeve and leg.

"I hardly think so."

"Well, we can try."

Before Michael Karl could protest the peasant's blouse was whipped over his head and his torn shirt was all that hid the Cross.

"You look as though you've been in a fight," commented the American.

"They weren't any too gentle about searching me," admitted Michael Karl.

The diamond Cross lay heavy. He wished with all his might that he had left it to share the Crown's hiding place in the Royal Train.

"Good Lord, what are you, a walking jewelry store?" The Cross had slipped through a rent in his shirt to catch the American's attention.

Michael Karl laughed wryly. "Just about that. One of my late master's possessions. He had no desire to let it fall into the Werewolf's paws even if he himself did, and as I had been searched and so was safe, I was elected to wear the thing. I'm to take it to Rein and turn it over to some one in authority. The thing's a nuisance."

He pulled it off and handed it to the American. If he acted the role of frankness it would bolster up his story of being an imposed-upon American aide-de-camp of the Prince.

"I've seen this somewhere before," his host declared. Michael Karl's eyes narrowed. "I know, it was on display with the Crown jewels at some sort of a benefit. One paid half a gruden and went in to see the Crown jewels and the coronation robes and things. The money went to charity. There was some sort of a legend about this. One of these arrows is supposed to be hollow and contain a sliver of one of the arrows which made Sebastian a martyr. The thing is only worn by the Crown Prince, a curse rests on it for any one else."

"Then I'm in for it," sighed Michael Karl. "Well, curse, do your stuff." He fastened the chain around his neck again and allowed its brilliance to dangle down upon the pajama coat the American had urged him into.

"By the way, what is your name? I don't like to go on saying 'you' all the time," he said as he tucked the Cross out of sight.

The American smiled oddly. "I'm Frank Ericson, and you?"

Michael Karl was ready for that question. Drawing from his stock of seven names he replied glibly: "John Stephenson. And now we're introduced."

Frank Ericson laughed and went to answer a rap on the door. He was back a moment later to prop Michael Karl up with pillows and settle a tray burdened with steaming dishes on his knees.

"This," said Michael Karl with no little satisfaction when the secrets of various covered dishes were laid bare before him, "is what I call a meal. You don't know what I've been through these last two months. It was don't eat this and don't eat that."

"But surely the meals of His Royal Highness's staff aren't supervised like that," protested the American.

Michael Karl hurried to retrieve his blunder. "Oh, but we couldn't have anything which was forbidden His Royal Highness. And everything good," declared Michael Karl, with some bitterness, through a full mouth, "was."

"What are you going to do now?" his host questioned as he lifted the empty tray off the bed a few minutes later.

"I'm going to slip out of here if I can, get into Rein to deliver this," he motioned towards the hidden Cross, "and sail for home on the next boat."

"Look here," interrupted Ericson, "I'm really a representative of an American newspaper up here to get the dope on this Werewolf. Now you can give me all the material I need, and I won't have to waste any more time pretending to climb mountains, when even to look out of a second-story window makes me dizzy. You come back to Rein with me. I can smuggle you in as my chauffeur, mine quit me cold when he found out where I was going. Do you have a passport?"

Michael Karl shook his head. "That was what I was worrying about," he confessed.

"Well, I know the American minister slightly, and I may be able to fix it up for you."

"But that's putting you to a lot of trouble," said Michael Karl doubtfully.

"Not at all," declared the American. "And the story you'll be able to give me will be worth every bit of it and more too. You will give me a story, won't you?" he stopped to ask anxiously.

"Everything I know about the Werewolf is yours," Michael Karl answered him promptly.

"Good!" The American was enthusiastic. "I'll go half on space rates. You'll bunk with me in town until the Minister can get your passport. We can see the fun when they're trying to ransom your boy friend. This sure has been a lucky day for me."

"And for me, too," said Michael Karl thankfully.

"And now, you're going to sleep, young fellow m'lad."

The two pillows behind Michael Karl were deftly pulled out and he was settled down comfortably. Just before the American blew out the candle he spoke again.

"If you need anything in the night, just call, I'm in the next room."

He went out softly and left Michael Karl staring at the dying fire on the hearth. A while ago he had been very tired, but now he was wide-awake. Providence or Fate or whatever was looking after him was certainly on the job.

The American attracted him, but he had a queer feeling that Frank Ericson wasn't any more the tall young man's name than John Stephenson was the name that he, Michael Karl, generally answered to. To be sure there was a "Johann" and a "Stefan" among the seven names with which they had loaded him at birth.

On the hearth the fire flickered and the shadows grew very long indeed. Michael Karl's eyes closed. For some reason he felt very happy, maybe it was because he was free at last.

There was a sharp click, and Michael Karl rolled over lazily to have the morning sun beat straight into his unguarded eyes. The American was standing at the open casement staring out.

"Really, must you be so energetic so early in the morning?" inquired Michael Karl somewhat peevishly. His shoulder was thumping, and his feet were hurrying to inform him that they were still there.

"Hullo! You've come to at last? It's past ten," Frank Ericson informed his guest with a smile.

Michael Karl sat up guiltily. "I say, it isn't!"

"But it is. And I'm afraid, if you are able, we must be on our way. I've been hearing things about our friend up yonder," he nodded curtly towards the window.

"I knew," Michael Karl said with some satisfaction, "that he wouldn't let me get away as easy as that. Well, I've got to be going then. If you can lend me a pair of shoes—"

"We're leaving in an hour," Ericson informed him. "And I've got your livery here. Remember, you're my chauffeur, lent me by the editor of Rein's leading newspaper."

"But," protested Michael Karl firmly, "I got myself into this mess, and I'm not going to drag you in after me. I'm leaving alone."

He scrambled stiffly out of bed and essayed to stand. A little white, he sank back on the bed. Unable to stand, much less walk a step, he was dependent upon the American whether or no.

"Now that you've got over that foolishness, suppose you eat your breakfast while I have a look at those feet of yours."

The American produced a loaded tray and his first-aid kit almost by magic.

"There," he said when the last bandage was wrapped, "that will do, I think. Heinrich's boots will be about two sizes too large, so they won't cause you any trouble as long as you obey orders and keep off your feet."

"But what will people think of a chauffeur who can't even stand, much less drive a car. You'll give the game away right there," Michael Karl was triumphant.

Ericson smiled down at him. "I'll do the driving, and we'll have a convincing story for the public, never fear. You are to do as you are told!"

Michael Karl digested that and then said:

"Well, what do you want me to do?"

The American was striding up and down the room tugging perplexedly at his black hair. Suddenly he stopped and came to perch on the foot of the wide bed.

"We've been mountain climbing," he began.

"You're not so far wrong there," broke in Michael Karl.

Ericson silenced him with a look and continued: "I slipped and you were pulled down for a nasty fall. It was my fault, and that's why I'm so anxious about you and must hurry you back to Rein. The landlord will give out that you're my guide, I've fixed that, and in Rein they'll think that you're some boy I've picked up in the mountains. Can you speak Morvanian?"

"A very little. Only what I've picked up these last two months. The Court speaks English, you know."

Ericson frowned. "Well, that will have to do. Remember, you're my guide and have had a fall on the rocks. Now let's get you into this."

He pulled out a pair of dark green breeches with a high-collared, side-buttoned tunic to match and pushed and pulled Michael Karl into them by main force. They fitted tolerably well except for the black boots, which as Ericson had said were too large, but they just went over the rolls of bandages.

"Not so bad," commented the American when he had finished and Michael Karl was established in a chair before the mirror. "You'd better put a strip of adhesive tape on that scratch of yours, it will add a little color to our story."

Michael Karl obeyed and then surveyed his reflection. The face in the mirror was a little pale perhaps and the splash of white plaster across one cheek gave him a slightly damaged appearance, but he sadly feared that any one who had seen the late Crown Prince would be very apt to recognize him. He'd have to lie close once he got to Rein. Do his errand with the Cross and then stick indoors until Ericson talked the American Minister into giving him a passport.

Ericson packed by the simple method of tossing all his clothes into two grips and pressing them down until the lids snapped together. An untidy but very swift method it proved. He pulled on a faded trench coat and a weather-beaten hat. Grabbing up both bags he started out the door.

"I'm going to bring the car around," he told Michael Karl, "and then Hans and I will be up to get you."

Michael Karl heard the exhaust of a car below and then some one clumped up the stairs. He hadn't had long to wait. Hans proved to be the stable boy, a bashfully grinning, tow-head youngster of about Michael Karl's age. He ducked his head in Michael Karl's general direction and stood waiting for orders.

The American came in like a whirlwind, and Michael Karl had the breathless feeling of one caught in such a storm. Hans under a volley of orders succeeded in aiding Michael Karl to his feet and partly leading, partly carrying him out of the door, across the landing and down the stairs.

The landlord, the "jelly" of the wolfman's disrespectful comment, stood smiling to bow them out, his pudgy hands playing with his none too clean apron. His smile was a little strained, and Michael Karl knew that for all the American's fine story, the landlord suspected who his sudden guest was and just who wanted him very badly.

They were out of the door into the Inn courtyard, and Michael Karl was carefully placed on the seat of a light gray roadster. Hans went away grinning bashfully still and fingering the first piece of silver he had seen in a long day. Wealthy travelers like this American were very few and far between at the Inn of the Crown.

The Inn sign, a warped and badly painted crown, creaked farewell and they were off with the American at the wheel. Michael Karl glanced back over his shoulder. He never expected to see the Inn of the Crown again.

"These roads," said his companion suddenly, "are preposterous. Near Rein there are none better even in America, but once you get ten miles beyond a city they're simply horrible."

He skillfully swerved to avoid a couple of large stones lying carelessly in the middle of the right of way.

"It wouldn't take one man ten minutes to cart those away, but no one has, and I'll bet they've been there more than a year. You'd think that the government would do something about it. They do have some sort of a road inspector but the job has a fat salary attached so it goes to some fool at court who's a friend of the higher ups. It's the same way with everything; that Werewolf for instance, if they really wanted to get rid of him they could, but there's too much graft."

The American's words set Michael Karl thinking. If he had ruled, how much could he have done towards straightening out the muddled affairs of the kingdom hampered by such aides as the Count and the General?

"Tell me about Rein," he commanded suddenly.

Michael Karl Enters His Capital

The American was only too eager to describe Michael Karl's capital.

"It's a wonderful place. The upper town hasn't been touched since the middle of the eighteenth century. Historians and such go quite wild about it. You know its history of course—"

"No," said Michael Karl, "I don't know any more about it than it's called Rein and is on the Laub river."

The American glanced at him sharply.

"Well, it was the ducal city when Morvania was a duchy instead of a kingdom. The Castle Fortress was built before and during the Crusades and the Cathedral in 1234. Morvania was a duchy until 1810 when the reining duke got the favor of Napoleon and had two large slices from neighboring states added to his duchy and the whole made a kingdom.

"It caused a lot of trouble because Innesberg was one of the small towns the Duke seized, and Innesberg is now almost as large as Rein and the leading commercial and manufacturing city in the kingdom. The place is a hotbed of Communism and the Council is going to have a lot of trouble with it before long. The last king was assassinated while visiting there. Innesberg has none of Rein's beauty or age and is shunned by the nobility. It is very modern and ugly.

"Rein on the other hand is like one of those improbably beautiful tower cities which appear now and then stamped on the covers of fairy tale books. The streets in the Upper Town are paved with cobblestones and most of them too narrow to get a car through. On the crown of the hill is the fortress and the Upper Town winds up to meet it.

"The New or Lower Town, where the foreign colony, Ministers, commercial representatives and so forth live, is across the Laub at the foot of the hill."

"Where do you live?" interrupted Michael Karl.

"A friend of mine lent me his house on the Pala Horn. It's a curving street leading out of the Cathedral Square. Only the more conservative of the older nobility live there now when even outsiders like myself creep in, but once only the bluest of the blue bloods dared to think of living there. My house is directly below the Fortress and there is a legend that a secret passage connects the two, a bolthole used by the duke in the old days.

"From the Cathedral Square there's a maze of little streets full of queer little shops and inns. And if you follow down far enough you come to the Bargo, the criminal section of town. The place is a horror and should be cleaned up.

"If instead of going straight down you follow the wide avenue which they call 'The Avenue of the

Duke' around the curve of the hill you come to the bridge which leads across the Laub to New Rein. New Rein and the Upper Town have little in common nowadays.

"But Rein is a stronghold in more ways than one. The saying goes, 'Who Holds Rein Holds Morvania,' and that is more than true. You see it's built at the apex of the triangle which is the fertile plain of Morvania. Innesberg is well out in the middle of the plain.

"Should Innesberg revolt, Rein can bring her to terms in no time at all. All Innesberg's water supply is pumped from the mountains behind Rein. A couple of bombs well placed would send the pipes miles high, and Innesberg would be very meek."

"What sort of an air force is there?"

The American frowned and then his face cleared. "Oh, bombing planes for the pipe job? Well, there's a wreck of a thing that the thrifty king bought after the last mixup. A wild country-man of ours risks his neck in it once a week or whenever the Council want to impress visiting dig-nitaries with the 'Air Force.' No, any bombing to be done would have to be done on the earth."

They rumbled over a wooden bridge. Mountains and their rolling foothills had given way to the pleasant level country where, here and there, a bright-coated peasant was urging a clumsy ox or heavy-footed horse on to plow his field. The moist furrows were very brown against the spring green of the grass, and the gayest of breezes was tugging at Michael Karl's leather peaked cap. It might be snowing in the mountains, but spring had come to stay in the farmlands.

He breathed deeply and wished somewhat wistfully that he could wander at will along the road. Ericson smiled sympathetically.

"It does get one, doesn't it? But wait until you see Rein for the first time. We come down the Hartiz Mountain, and the Laub looks like a silver chain holding the whole city in enchantment. There's nothing like it anywhere else on earth."

A shepherd, whose round cloth cap boasted the jauntiest of cock's feathers, whistled to his dog, and the gray roadster drew to one side to let the worried little collie snap and bark his stupid charges across the road. With a lazy smile the shepherd touched his cap and wished them a pleasant day and a fine ending to their journey.

"Half of Morvania's charm," Frank Ericson seemed to speak more to himself than to Michael Karl, "is her people. If they were only let alone they would be the happiest and most contented people in the world. But they aren't, they're too loyal. Morvania hasn't changed since the Middle Ages. They're loyal to death and beyond for some worthless cub—"

"Like the Crown Prince," murmured Michael Karl.

"Just so. He probably doesn't care a thing about them. All he wants is the throne and what he can get out of it. The Karloffs are noted for looking out for themselves first. What does he care about Morvania?"

"Maybe," began Michael Karl hesitatingly, "maybe he never wanted to rule, maybe he wants to be free to live his own life."

Ericson looked at Michael Karl somewhat sternly. "No one of Royal blood," he answered slowly, "is ever free. He has a certain duty, he is a soldier always on active service. If this Crown Prince was true to the service he would come here and clean out the whole mess of idlers and worse who have been living off the people and ruining the country. He would be king in fact as well as in name. There is a big job before him, but it is more than certain that he will shirk it."

"But," Michael Karl almost wailed, "he doesn't want to rule. He never wanted to come to Morvania; they practically dragged him here."

"I said," repeated the American, "that he wasn't big enough for the job. He's selfish like all of his line."

Michael Karl thought furiously. Was he selfish? Was it his duty to rule the country? Would he be a deserter if he slipped out of Morvania on a forged passport and left the country to the General, the Count, and their following? He had never looked at that side of it before.

Ericson was talking of something else, "He has something more to do, this Crown Prince. His cousin, the rightful heir, died in the mountains—how?"

"Black Stefan," answered Michael Karl promptly, at least he was sure of that. But the American shook his head.

"Why do you suppose I came into the mountains?" he asked and then answered his own question swiftly. "Because I heard a very queer story about Prince Urlich Karl. I don't know whether you know the laws of Morvania or not, but this is what happened. When a King dies suddenly and the heir does not claim the throne within seven days, the control of the government passes to the Council of Nobles for one year. At the end of that time the heir must claim the throne or another heir be found."

"Why didn't Urlich Karl claim the throne?"

"He was—prevented!"

"How?"

"By certain of the Nobles. He was on an hunting trip when his grandfather, the old king, was killed. The news reached him and he started back for Rein. On the way he disappeared, and the Council of Nobles got control."

"But what happened?" demanded Michael Karl.

The American answered him with one word, "Murder!"

"Black Stefan—" began Michael Karl; he was still bewildered.

"Black Stefan had nothing to do with it," answered the American almost savagely, "in fact—" but he did not finish his sentence.

"The Council—" ventured Michael Karl somewhat timidly.

"The Council." And the American's tone was grim.

"You see," he explained after a moment, "I knew Urlich Karl."

They drove on in silence. Michael Karl was frowning into the reflecting windshield; somehow it was no longer so easy to think of leaving the Cross and slipping away to America. Urlich Karl must have been rather the right sort, for suddenly Michael Karl knew that this new friend of his

would like only the right sort. And when Frank
Ericson talked of Urlich Karl, he made a person
want to go out and shoot the General and the
Count and the rest of the Council.

The road was climbing again, and they left the
level farmlands behind them. As Ericson had said,
the poor paving of the early miles had disappeared
and they were making good time on smooth con-
crete.

"Rein is over the mountain," remarked Ericson
as the roadster started the steady pull.

"And here," he said a moment later, "is where
we stop for passport inspection. Now remember
you're a dumb youngster I picked up in the mountains."

They slowed down before a whitewashed stone
hut in the curve of the road. At the sound of their
engine a black-uniformed soldier stepped smartly
out; to his horror Michael Karl recognized the uniform as that of his own regiment. What if the
fellow had seen a picture of him?

He slipped down in the seat as far as he could
and was thankful that Ericson was between him
and the inspector.

"Your passport, yes?" The soldier smiled pleasantly and held out his hand for the bundle of
papers.

"And this is your chauffeur?" he tried to get a
better look at Michael Karl, but almost by chance
the American leaned forward at the same time so
all he could see was one dark green coat sleeve.

He ruffled the papers together again and
handed them back. "You had better keep them at

hand, sir, there are patrols out between here and the city."

"What's happened?" asked the American.

The soldier frowned. "It is not permitted to ask," he replied shortly and waved them on.

"Then they haven't told what happened to the Crown Prince," Michael Karl was excited.

"They don't dare. If anything happens to this candidate for the throne, the Council will be left holding the bag and the Communists will make hay. They're making a still hunt for the Prince hoping to get by without the people learning what's the matter," explained the American.

Then he had a better chance then ever, thought Michael Karl. They didn't dare hunt for him openly. He wished though that they would catch the Werewolf. Usually he didn't wish anybody bad luck, but he had no brotherly feeling for the Werewolf after that meeting in the hall.

Ericson slowed down and finally came to a stop at a cleared place in the forest.

"Look down," he commanded.

Far below a river twisted about the base of a tall rock-like hill and reflected a thousand times the spires and towers of a gray city built upon the rock's crown these hundreds of years. Above the city itself was the Fortress Castle of the kings, and even as they watched a colored standard was raised to crack in the high wind from the peak of a tower.

"The City of Rein," said the American softly with a queer note in his voice.

Michael Karl stared down, studying every detail

of the city below and thought that the American was right, Rein had an enchantment all its own, so much was it like the fairy city that Ericson had compared it to.

"There's another hour before we cross the old bridge," Ericson said at last as he started the motor. "Well, what do you think of Rein?"

"It is very beautiful," said Michael Karl soberly.

They started down the mountain road and for the first time met fellow travelers. It was a road of contrasts between the old world and the new: a smart sport roadster of the latest model, guided by a laughing officer who blew the horn furiously until a two-wheeled ox cart crawled out to give it room to pass, flashed by a peasant in a scarlet blouse and round cap who was plodding steadily along under a heavy bag, on his way to the markets of Rein. It was all new and rather exciting.

The patrol did not appear to stop them, and they were in sight of the bridge in less than the hour Ericson had promised. A soldier snapped to attention as they pulled onto the ancient stone paving.

"He's saluting that crest on the car door not us," the American informed Michael Karl. "As I told you these people are feudal in their ideas. This car belongs to one of the great lords and landowners who is a good friend of mine. That guard probably came from his section of the country."

"Look at the flowers!" Michael Karl leaned over the door to see them closer. The whole side of the bridge was covered like a small rainbow with blue, violet, orange, all shades from pink to deepest crimson, flowers. And among them, peasant girls, looking like old-fashioned bouquets of their own sweets in their brilliant skirts and shoulder shawls, were busy arranging and marketing the blossoms.

"The old flower market," said Ericson with a smile. "It has been held here daily for a hundred years or more. Of course it is beautiful now, but later in the year it is one of the most wonderful sights in Morvania. There," a scarlet rose brushed Michael Karl's cheek and dropped into his lap, "you seem to be making a hit with the ladies."

Michael Karl glared fiercely at the laughing girl who had thrown it.

"Drive on!" he snapped.

The American laughed, and they were over the bridge and climbing a cobble-paved street. The houses, with every story added to their height, jutted out farther over the pavement, until, as Michael Karl glimpsed in an alley they shot by, they sometimes met over head.

"This is the perfect setting for the *Three Musketeers*," Ericson pointed toward the beamed and plastered houses. "Can't you picture them roughing it down this street on their way to have it out with the Cardinal's guards?

"And this is the vegetable market," he said a moment later as they entered a busy square. Like the flower market it glowed with the scarlet, gold and red of early vegetables.

"Not much of a show now, but a month from now it will be quite a sight. I wish you could see the animal market but we can't drive through there. When you are able to walk we'll go."

They threaded their way out of the vegetable

market and up and down the dark streets until Michael Karl was completely bewildered. All at once they came out upon an impressive square dominated by a great Cathedral.

"The Cathedral Square," announced the American. "We must see that too," he pointed to the Cathedral.

Michael Karl thought privately that he wasn't going to have much time for sight-seeing and he wasn't going to be able to go about too openly. The Prince looked back at the Cathedral; it was pretty impressive, but he'd probably never see it any closer. He didn't foresee, for how could he, the Battle of the Cathedral Steps.

Out of the Cathedral Square into a proud avenue of stately homes they went. Above every door all the fabled monsters of heraldry winked or blinked, and family coats-of-arms were carved, to be pitted by the sand-filled wind which came roaring up from the Lower Town in winter time.

"Here we are." The roadster stopped at last before a house in the middle of the row. As if he had been at watch for their coming, as indeed he had, a roundish little man with close-clipped gray hair appeared like a jack-in-the-box on the door steps and came hastening down to greet them.

"Dominde, Dominde!" he cried excitedly, rubbing his hands together.

"Hello, Jan, and how goes things?" asked Ericson stepping out stiffly.

"Very well, Dominde," beamed the little man.

"That is good. And now if you will summon Breck and Kanda, my friend has had an accident and will have to be helped in."

"Of course, of course, Dominde." The little man clucked like a hen and looked at Michael Karl pityingly as he turned back to the house. In no time at all he was back like a fussy, too-plump tug with a couple of six-foot steamers of footmen in tow.

With the help of Breck and Kanda Michael Karl was brought in and comfortably established before an open fire in the library of the house. Still a little dazed by the magnificence of the footmen's powdered heads and rich livery, and the stateliness of the apartment he found himself in, Michael Karl settled back to see what would happen next.

Jan popped in, followed by Kanda with a tray. "I thought, Dominde," he began rather humbly, "that you might require refreshment after your journey."

The silent Kanda placed the tray on the desk, and they bowed themselves out together. Ericson lounged over to inspect the tray. "Coffee and—milk. That must be for you, the efficient Jan would never dare bring me milk," he smiled down at Michael Karl, and Michael Karl grinned back.

"I suppose you expect me to get all hot and bothered over Jan thinking me young enough to enjoy milk, but I do. So you can just hand it over, Mr. Man."

And Michael Karl sipped from the tall glass while the American glanced through the pile of letters on his desk. He did it very untidily, letting the opened envelopes drift to the floor instead of putting them in the basket by his side, Michael Karl noted with disapproval.

"What am I doing now?" Ericson asked suddenly. Michael Karl flushed as he realized that he had been staring at his host.

"I was thinking," he said ruefully, "what my guardian would have done to me if I had thrown papers around like that. Though I'm not denying that it's a relief to do it sometimes."

"You're a very orderly person aren't you, John Stephenson?" asked the American. His eyes had their amused look. "But you see I was brought up to throw things around and have some one pick them up for me. Perhaps if I had had your guardian instead of"—he checked himself quickly.

"You wouldn't have liked my guardian—" began Michael Karl to cover the pause. He wondered what Ericson had been about to say.

"That reminds me, hadn't you better cable him that you are all right? He'll probably learn through the newspapers of the Crown Prince's capture and he will be worrying."

"My guardian," replied Michael Karl with some truth, "washed his hands of me when I started on this fool trip."

Ericson looked at him with some surprise. "I can hardly believe that, but I suppose it's so. And now you're going to bed."

"But it isn't even noon yet," protested Michael Karl.

"Those feet of yours are going to get their chance to rest."

So Breck and Kanda were sent for again and Michael Karl found himself in a room which he thought would be a comfortable size for a Union Station but was far too large for a bedroom. And in spite of all his protests he was, fifteen minutes later, half sitting, half lying in a bed big enough for one of the small steamers. It could, he discovered after experimenting, be shut off from the room by heavy crimson velvet curtains.

"How do you like it?" asked the American from the door. He crossed the room to dump a couple of books and three of the reddest apples Michael Karl had ever seen on the bed. "Something to keep you busy," he commented as Michael Karl examined his spoils.

"It's very nice," said Michael Karl looking about him, "but don't you think that it's rather on the large side?"

"This is very small compared to the Royal bedroom in the Palace. I think a whole army could comfortably hold maneuvers there."

Jan poked his gray head around the corner of the door. "Dominde," he said in his humble voice, "the telephone demands your attendance."

"Sorry. If there's anything you want, ring." Ericson looped the velvet bell cord in reach of Michael Karl's hand and hurried out.

Michael Karl picked up the books. *The History of Rein Fortress*, he read aloud, *The History of the Karloffs in Rein*.

He put them down and frowned uncertainly. Did the American—guess anything? Why had they left the Inn so suddenly when Michael Karl had been assured that it was perfectly safe to stay, and why had the American delivered that little speech about the duty of Royalty as if he had known that Michael Karl was planning to—well, desert? And now these books about Rein and the Karloffs. Michael Karl shook his head. He wasn't going to worry about the future. Well, not just yet, at least.

Snuggling back into his pillows he selected the reddest and hardest of the apples to sink his teeth into while he opened *The History of Rein Fortress*, and began to read.

Chapter VI

Of A Chance Discovery And A Passage
Underground

"What are you doing?"

Michael Karl looked up guiltily from piling the peeling of his breakfast orange in a topheavy tower. "I'm thinking," he answered soberly.

He had been up and about, only hobbling to be sure, for the past two days and it was a week since his surprising adventures in the mountains.

"And do you always frown so horribly when you are thinking?" inquired Ericson.

"Was I frowning?" asked Michael Karl in some surprise.

"If you don't believe me, go and think in front of a mirror and see what happens. And what were you thinking about?"

"How I am going to return the Cross without being seen."

"Are you going to return it?"

Michael Karl was startled. "Of course. Why not?"

The American looked away. "Oh, just an idea of mine. Thought that you'd like to return it to its owner when he's ransomed."

"I never want to see the Crown Prince again,"
said Michael Karl in a low voice, his fingers busy
with the bits of peeling.

"Are you sure?" There was an odd note in the
American's voice, and again Michael Karl wondered just how much or how little his host really
knew.

"Yes," answered Michael Karl firmly and de-
molished his tower with a sweep of his hand.

"What are you going to do to-day?" Ericson
asked a moment later. There was a faint trace of
disappointment in his voice as if he had looked for
something long hoped for and found it missing.
Michael Karl felt queerly to blame, but he wasn't
going to give up his new-found freedom for a
friend's disappointment if that was what the
American had hoped for.

"Oh, I don't know," he answered carelessly.
"The usual thing I suppose. There isn't much I can
do now."

"I'm going to be busy in the library. I wish you'd
go out a little."

Michael Karl shook his head. "Too many know
me, I can't risk being seen. I'll attempt it to-night
after dark. I'm going to get my books out of the
library. You're not to be disturbed this morning I
suppose?"

"No. Do you know, you're making me a mighty
fine secretary, John. I wish I could persuade you
to stay on. I'd never got all that material ready for
the article on Morvanian witchcraft if it hadn't
been for your help."

Michael Karl folded his napkin and arose to his

feet. "My dear sir, I am overwhelmed," he said with an excellent imitation of his late aide-de-camp's heel clicking bow. "And now to work. I shall be in the anteroom as usual if you need me."

The American smiled with lazy admiration. "Keeping the old man to it, aren't you? You hurry away from the breakfast table all full of zeal because you know it will shame me into working too. Some morning I'm going to defy you and sit right here for another cup of coffee. I wonder if you're so busy when I'm not watching you?"

"Pop in and see," suggested Michael Karl.

Ericson shook his head. "I couldn't, that squeaky board in the hall would always warn you in time. You go over the mail this morning and answer everything you can. I hate to write letters, and you seem to enjoy it so you might as well answer mine. Don't interrupt me unless the palace burns down or something. And don't let Jan in to tell some tale of woe, you handle him.

"And don't worry about the Cross," he added as he opened the library door. "I'll find some way for you to return it."

Michael Karl seated himself before the table in the anteroom. It was interesting work, this answering of mail and reading up of history to help his host, and it made him feel that he was not quite so useless. He wished that he might accept the American's offer and stay on as a secretary.

Jan appeared with the morning mail and laid it carefully on the table. The little man always carried the mail basket as if it contained something breakable.

"Good morning, Dominde," he smiled humbly

and backed out, bowing very low at Michael Karl's hearty answer.

The mail went into two piles, those private and those pertaining to business, but it was a long green envelope which excited all Michael Karl's interest this morning. Ericson had told him about these green envelopes, but this was the first time he had seen one. It never came by post, but was delivered by hand and was not to be opened, but to be taken to the American sealed.

Wondering about it, he pushed it into the table drawer for safe keeping and went about answering the rest. As Ericson said, Michael Karl liked to write letters, perhaps because he had never written any before, and was developing a flair for the difficult business. He seemed to know by instinct what to say and how to say it.

The volume of the American's mail often surprised him. There were so many letters from such queer people. Every one seemed to know that Ericson was collecting unusual facts about the country and its customs, he wanted to do a sort of travel book about Morvania, and they wrote in things that they knew.

A horse trader in this morning's mail had sent in a long description of some odd points about his trade in the northern mountains. He seemed to be an educated man who noticed everything and Michael Karl enjoyed his letter, and ended by putting it in the basket marked "To be Filed," for the American kept files of all sorts of odds and ends of information.

There was a badly spelt and written letter,

accompanied by a crude map, all about a little known pass over the Laub Mountains, which joined the horse trader's letter after a careful and more legible copy had been made and clipped to the original.

One or two circulars from advertising companies were put aside, for Michael Karl had learned that while Ericson allowed him to answer almost all letters he was not to throw away any until the American had seen them.

The mail was opened and a rough draft of the answer was carefully pinned to each letter, for the typewriter was in the library, and Michael Karl had to wait until noon before he could enter. He believed that Ericson spent the morning working on his book, for he always disappeared in there at nine o'clock and did not come out until twelve, during which time he kept the door locked and every one was forbidden entrance.

Michael Karl piled the letters neatly and turned to his books. At the American's suggestion he was studying the mountain dialect of Morvania, going over each morning's study with Kanda who was a mountaineer. Also he was reading the history of Rein. The books Ericson had lent him during his enforced stay in bed had given him the desire to learn more about the ancient capital of Morvania.

He was deep in the mysteries of an irregular verb when Jan came timidly in.

"Dominde, Dominde Ericson has gone out, he says that you may use the library now if you wish."

Michael Karl glanced at the clock on the mantel.

"But it's only ten-thirty," he said in surprise. Ericson had always used the library until twelve before.

"The Dominde was suddenly called away."

"All right." Michael Karl laid down his book and shuffled his papers together.

There was a fire burning in the library though the month was May, for these stone-walled houses of the Upper Town with their backs tight against the Fortress rock were cool and damp even on the warmest of days. Michael Karl spread out his papers on the American's clean desk; as untidy as he was in most things, the top of Frank Ericson's desk was always kept neat. Although Michael Karl suspected that he just opened one of the drawers and brushed things in when he was ready to leave.

His fingers flew over the keyboard of the typewriter. Typewriting was the one modern accomplishment which for some reason the Colonel had ordered him taught. Probably he did it because Michael Karl was the only one who could read Michael Karl's handwriting. The clock struck half past eleven when he finished the last letter and laid them all carefully on the desk awaiting Ericson's scrawled signature.

He still had the horse trader and mountaineer letters to file and a list to make of all the informative letters which had come in that week. And he was busy at that task when Jan summoned him to lunch. It was not until he passed through the anteroom on his way to the dining room that he remembered the green envelope.

The table drawer was perhaps not the safest place for it. He held it in his hand and looked around, if he could carry it with him— His boots! It wouldn't be the first time he had concealed something in the tops of his boots. He still had on Heinrich's too large ones which made it all the better. Michael Karl tucked the green envelope into the top of his riding boot.

He was still wearing the green breeches and tunic which had been given him in the Crown Inn. None of Ericson's clothes would fit him, and in these he could better keep up the fiction of being some sort of a secretary chauffeur.

The American was not there for lunch but that was nothing unusual, he didn't eat more than half of his meals at the house. Michael Karl tasted the spicy dishes with some satisfaction. He was growing to like Morvanian cooking so well that Ericson had laughingly warned him about his waistline.

Feeling well fed, drowsy, and very much at peace with the world Michael Karl limped back to the library. He was safe from all but unexpected interruptions until four when Jan would bustle in with the afternoon tea, and Ericson would lounge in to pour himself the cup he never drank and sit telling Michael Karl interesting things about his day's work until his tea cooled and he ordered it taken away in disgust. In all the time Michael Karl had been there he had never seen the American drink his tea.

The list of the week's letters had been made, neatly copied and laid on Ericson's desk for his attention, and Michael Karl felt free to return to his language studies. He had a method all his own for the learning of irregular verbs which he was using this afternoon. One said the verb over three or four times looking at the book and then the book was put aside. Fixing his eyes firmly on the opposite wall, Michael Karl would try to picture the word spelled out letter by letter on its polished surface.

"I-a-g—g— What does come next?" Michael Karl sternly repressed the desire to look in the book and began again. "I-A-G—" But again it refused to form under his eyes. Perhaps that corner in the panel made too much of a shadow and so distracted his attention. Why that was queer, none of the other panels had that odd shadowed corner in them.

He laid down his book and crossed the room. The shadow in the panel provoked his curiosity. Why, part of the wall was sticking out! With his finger nails he caught and tugged at the edge. Something gave way and the whole panel swung out noiselessly like a door.

It must be the secret passage of which Ericson had told him. Without thinking he boldly clambered through. On a shelf beside the door lay a flashlight. Then Ericson or some one in the house used the passage and used it often enough to leave the light there.

Michael Karl remembered things which had puzzled him, Ericson's intimate knowledge of the palace and its inhabitants for instance. He hesitated—would it be exactly playing the game to follow the passage and learn its secret? If Ericson had wanted him to know about it wouldn't he have told him?

And then he thought of the Cross. What better way of returning it unseen than to use the secret passage? He examined the inner fastening of the panel so that he would be sure to get it open again and picked up the torch. As the panel clicked shut behind him he felt a little tingle of excitement run up his back. He was off adventuring again.

The passage ran straight for a couple of yards and then ended in a flight of narrow stone steps. Michael Karl eyed them doubtfully, his feet were apt even now to protest when tried too much. But the excitement of adventure made him try it.

The air in the passage was chill but fresh and there was none of the dank sliminess which Michael Karl had always associated with underground passages. He must be inside the mountain itself, climbing the distance between the Pala Horn and the Palace Fortress.

The stairs were bisected suddenly by a deep landing. There was the outline of a door on the right wall and in it an inch above the level of Michael Karl's eyes the narrow slit of a peephole. He stretched on tiptoe to use it. But all he could see was dense darkness, and the distant sound of water made him think that this door led into the ancient dungeons.

There were more stairs after he left the dungeon door, but no more landings and at last he found himself at the top of the stairs in a long narrow hall. A crack of light, again to his right, showed him a second door and peephole. This time he looked into a wide hall with a marble stairway and crimson carpet, which took his breath away with their splendor. From the American's stories he identified it with the stairway leading to the throne room.

Beside a farther door there was a pair of powdered footmen who far surpassed Breck and Kanda in gorgeousness, and a wooden sentry pacing back and forth. He waited a while to see if anything would happen but the sentry was as stiff as ever and the footmen just stood, so Michael Karl went on.

The scene from the next peephole showed him what seemed to be a gun room. He was greatly tempted to try this door and step out a second or two to examine the ancient swords and guns in the wall racks but his prudence won. From the gun room steps led up again. Michael Karl began to think that this secret passage was overprovided with stairs.

When the next beam of light betrayed a peephole to him, he had no idea where he was. The secret door seemed to be some distance from the floor and his view was somewhat curtailed by the back of a tall chair. Then he understood he was in the throne room behind the throne itself!

The room was deserted and this time Michael Karl's curiosity won. He pushed down on the lever at the side and the door slipped back. Michael Karl wondered at its noiselessness until his hand came away greasy from the lever. The door had been recenty oiled. But, of course, the American must come and go through all the doors at his will. Michael Karl stepped out, leaving the door ajar behind him; he pulled a thick fold of the crimson velvet hangings into the crack as a further safe-guard against its closing.

The vacant throne was the most impressive thing he had ever seen. It stood on a four-step dais under a crimson canopy with a silver standard draped over its back. He knew that to be the Royal Standard which followed the king into battle.

For a moment he was tempted to seat himself as was his right, and then he shook his head. It wasn't his right any more, he had given that up as the price of his freedom. With a little sigh, perhaps half of regret, he looked down the long room with its chandeliers of crystal and gold.

The walls were painted with scenes from Morvanian history. Michael Karl had never seen the Hall of Mirrors, but at that moment he was sure, with a fierce pride, that nothing at Versailles could surpass the Throne Room of Rein Castle. He stood for a moment before the throne. Just so he might have stood in the glory of a white and gold hussar's uniform on the day of his coronation had he chosen to. But that, decided Michael Karl sternly, was past. Turning back to the passage he clicked the door shut behind him.

After the Throne Room, the black paneled room shown through the next peephole seemed small and mean for all its long table and seven high-backed chairs. Michael Karl thought, rightly, that it was some sort of a council chamber. There was no one there now and it didn't interest him. He went on, trying to remember where he had seen something which had given him the same queer feeling of power that the throne had impressed upon him. At last he remembered—the Werewolf's cloak-draped chair in the ruined castle. There was the same air of royal splendor and might about it as about the crimson canopied gold throne. Why?

He puzzled over that "why" until the passage came to an abrupt end before him. This time the peephole and the door were in the end instead of at the side.

Michael Karl saw a deep bed hung in crimson and embroidered in gold thread with the royal arms many times repeated. So this was the end of the old duke's bolthole, his bedroom. But, of course, at any sudden night alarm he might save his skin without trouble, and with what he had read and heard about his ancestors almost every one of them might have been driven to saving their skins at any moment. They had been a precious lot, the old Karloffs.

Like the Throne Room the bedroom aroused his curiosity to the point where he could no longer resist it. He stepped out and brought the door almost closed behind him, but wedged his handkerchief in to keep it open. For as yet he didn't know how to open the doors from the outside.

The rug under foot was thick and gray with the royal crest in red at its four corners. There were a couple of chests, museum pieces, and the massive bed where the crimson velvet upper cover had been turned back, as if waiting for the royal occupant, to show the sheerest of satin sheets and pillows trimmed in priceless lace. Michael Karl shuddered. What he had escaped! The somber magnificence of the room was suffocating.

Greatly daring he tiptoed across and pulled

open one of the doors an inch or two. It led into a
dressing room which was empty. Michael Karl
crossed it softly to open the farther door. It was a
wardrobe room, holding, to his dazed eyes, what
seemed like hundreds and hundreds of all colors
and kinds of uniforms. He closed it quickly. So
that was more of what he had escaped.

Michael Karl hurried back to the bedroom. The
other door he found upon investigation led into a
reception room. Without the tall window the afternoon light was fading, and he was dreadfully
afraid that it was past four o'clock. He stepped
back to the secret door. To his relief it was still
open, he had been haunted by the fear that it
might have slammed shut in spite of his handkerchief.

Did he or did he not hear some sort of a rustling
noise as he stepped into the passage? His nerves
were probably on edge from excitement he decided as he hurried down the hall. If it were anything it would only be a rat.

The stairs tired him more than he thought. He
would be glad to sit quietly the rest of the evening.
Back again outside the panel in Ericson's house he
listened until he thought the pounding blood in his
head would break his ear drums. Michael Karl had
no desire to show Ericson that he had discovered
his secret by stepping through the secret door before the American's very eyes. And here, unfortunately, was no peephole.

At last when he could stand it no longer he took
a chance and bore down upon the lever. The door
swung open. Michael Karl caught a confused
glimpse of Jan's coat tails disappearing through

the door. The tea tray was on the desk, and the room was empty.

Jan would think he had been out for a moment. With a sigh of relief Michael Karl brushed a cobweb from his shoulder and allowed the panel to click shut behind him. He crossed to the desk and put his afternoon's work carefully away before he sat down with a well-sweetened cup of tea in one hand and his grammar in the other to learn his irregular verb.

"Hello, youngster. Still busy?"

Michael Karl regarded the American with a somewhat glassy eye. "Iagio, iagiar, iagiari," he repeated.

Ericson reached over and took the book out of Michael Karl's hand.

"See here," he said, "I don't propose to have my afternoon tea spoiled by you repeating that stuff. Chuck it awhile. Busy all afternoon?"

Was it Michael Karl's imagination or was the American watching him closely? He thought swiftly. "Of course." After all he had been busy but in a different way.

"Hard work?"

"Not very. Oh, I say," Michael Karl remembered the green envelope. He reached down at his boot top. Funny, it had been right at the top, maybe it had slipped down though. He thrust his fingers farther down in and felt for the stiff paper. The green envelope was gone! It lay somewhere along his afternoon journeyings. He flushed.

"Yes?" prompted Ericson.

Michael Karl simply couldn't tell him. You couldn't say to a man who had practically saved your life, "See here, that letter you wanted came this morning but I lost it exploring your secret passage." Michael Karl felt a dull lump of sickness go sliding down in his breast. He had muffed things for fair; his one chance would be to go through the passage again to-night and try to recover the thing. Meanwhile he wanted to get away from the American and his questions.

"What did you want?" asked the American. "Boy, are you ill?"

Michael Karl's face was very white.

"I have a headache. I guess I'll go to bed," he said miserably. He wanted to get away and think this thing out. Hobbling across the room which seemed miles long he went out, knowing that the American was staring after him.

The stairs went up and up endlessly he thought. And after he reached his room he had the desire to sit down and howl. He felt as he hadn't since the night nine years before when the Colonel had taken a stray dog he had adopted from him.

Chapter VII

The Council At Work

Michael Karl lay in a tangle of sheets wondering how long it would be before he could attempt the passage again. As he had just crawled into bed and the clock below had just boomed five, it was apt to be several hours.

There was a knock at the door. Michael Karl didn't answer. He must keep up his fiction of being ill and if he kept still perhaps the knocker would think he had fallen asleep and go away.

But that was just what the knocker didn't do.

"What's the matter, boy?" Michael Karl, hearing the American's voice, felt more of a beast than ever. Ericson was really concerned, he only called Michael Karl "boy" when he wanted to praise or was worried about him.

"Nothing," the answer was very much muffled in the bedclothes. The American, standing beside him, caught another scrap of sentence about "headache" and "sleep it off."

He took Michael Karl firmly by the shoulder and turned him around so he could see the boy's flushed face.

"Don't be foolish. There is something the matter. You were all right up until a few minutes ago. Then after you started to tell me something you developed this sudden headache. What happened this afternoon?"

Michael Karl began to see that he had overplayed his role. It was going to be very hard to lie to the American. And, something inside of him said, he didn't want to anyway.

"Nothing," he answered again in a small voice which sounded bitterly ashamed in his own ears.

The American shrugged. "Well, if you won't tell me, you won't I suppose. But I did think—"

The way he allowed his sentence to trail off unfinished hurt more than any words could have. Ericson was disappointed in him, and all at once Michael Karl knew that he cared more for the American's friendship than anything else in the world.

"There was something," he said without meaning to. "I can't tell you now—"

But the American had gone. Michael Karl rolled over. If anything could have made him more miserable, it was that silent going. Ericson hadn't heard what he was going to say. He wished he had never seen that letter or been reckless enough to enter the secret door.

He was not going to think of Ericson he told himself sternly. But why had the American asked about how he had spent his afternoon? He had never done that before.

Suppose, Michael Karl caught his breath, suppose Ericson had known that he had used the passage and was waiting to see if he would " 'fess up." Why didn't he? It couldn't be any worse than it was now and the American would have his letter. It might be frightfully important.

Michael Karl reached for the bell cord and then he shook his head. He would go down and face Ericson in that fatal library. With clumsy fingers he pulled on shirt, breeches and boots and hurried out into the hall.

He sped down the stairs, but the library was empty. Feeling queerly sick as if he had missed a step in the dark he summoned Jan with a pull of the bell cord. He was a coward and he knew it.

"The Dominde Ericson," he demanded, "where is he?"

The little man seemed troubled. "The Dominde went out," he answered slowly, but there seemed to be something on his mind. Michael Karl thought he was nerving himself to ask a question, but he couldn't quite make it and he bowed himself out his question unasked.

So Ericson had gone out. Then there was a chance that he might enter the passage, find the letter, and return before Ericson. He almost ran to the wall but this time there was no jutting corner to guide him and he didn't know how to work the releasing spring. Well, he'd have to learn and do it quick.

Michael Karl closed the library door and locked it. Jan and the rest would think that their master had returned and was busy.

He went back to study the wall. The door panel was fifth from the fireplace and sixth from the corner of the room. Five and six made eleven, but that didn't mean anything, or did it? Each panel was carved with a bunch of grapes.

Everything that he had ever read about secret doors suggested that the grapes had something to do with the spring. Michael Karl counted the separate grapes carefully, if there were eleven on the bunch of the secret panel— There were but the same was true of the neighboring panels on either side.

It was like one of those bewildering field fortification problems which the Colonel used to torture him with. Given: one panel, eleven grapes, two leaves and a crooked stem. To find: the spring of a secret door. He pushed and pulled at each one of the grapes and then tried all combinations of grapes and leaves he could think of, but the door remained as fast set as ever.

Then he turned his attention to those panels on either side. It was when he looked at them closely that he discovered his first clue. On the one sixth from the fireplace five of the grapes were carved almost in a straight line, while on the one seventh from the corner of the room the grapes in a line numbered six. Taking a chance he pushed down on the fifth and the sixth grapes. There was a familiar click, and the secret door swung open.

The flashlight was on the shelf where he had left it and he stopped only to snatch it up before he started slowly along the passage and up the stairs allowing his light to penetrate into every corner of the stone steps. He passed the dungeon door and the door of the hall but nowhere did he see the slip of green.

At the throne room he halted and snapped open the door. He must search around the throne itself.

The room was dark and he had to shelter the torch with his hand for fear of discovery as he crept about on his knees. Beyond discovering several rolls of gray dust which testified to the palace's poor housekeeping there was nothing for him to see.

Rather frightened—somehow he had been sure that he had dropped the letter by the throne—he crawled back into the passage. There was the rest of the hall and the king's bedroom to go over, he must find that letter.

He came to the end of the passage without seeing so much as a hint of green and hesitated before the door to the bedroom. If he didn't find it here what was he going to do?

The door opened to his touch and he was on the gray carpet again. Over and under the great bed and the chests his torch poked and pried with no result.

"Well, there's the dressing room and the wardrobe yet," he tried to hearten himself aloud.

The dressing room was empty and he caught his breath as he stood before the wardrobe door. If he didn't find it inside, he was through. He opened the door an inch at a time afraid to look.

The beam from his torch sped along the polished floor until it caught and held a scrap of green paper. Michael Karl snatched the paper up eagerly and thrust it inside his shirt. He remembered at last how he had bent down to count the pairs of boots lined against the wall—it must have been then that he lost it.

Seeing the boots again gave him an idea. Since he had left off the last of his bandages that morning Heinrich's loose boots had become something of a problem. These boots had been made to his measure in preparation for his coming, why not help himself? Michael Karl selected the pair nearest to hand, a pair of tall campaign boots like those the American had cut off him, and sat down on a dressing room chair to pull them on.

They fit perfectly, but he would have to pay for them. He pulled a handful of grimy bills from his pocket. Thank goodness the American had lent him these. Ten gruden would surely be a fair price, anyway it was all he could afford. Laying the money down on the table, he picked up his torch and went out.

Michael Karl slipped through the secret door and was back in the passage, almost light-hearted again when he moved and heard the soft crackle of the paper beneath his shirt. He could face the American with a clear conscience and tell the whole story. Though, he thought with a wry face, the telling of it was going to be hard.

He had time to notice something now which had escaped his attention when he came up. There was a light in the room he had named the Council Chamber, and through the secret door he could hear the murmur of voices.

Standing on tiptoe he looked in. The seven chairs were occupied and the table was snowed under by a heap of official looking papers. Michael Karl's old friend, the Count, presided while the General puffed and blew, his red face redder than ever, at the Count's black elbow. There was a stiff, brown-faced man with the air of a soldier, whose bushy eyebrows and cold eyes reminded Michael

Karl of his old terror, the Colonel, at the Count's left. Next to the soldier was an effeminate youngster in a green and gold uniform which did not become his chinless, yellow face and lizard eyes. He did not seem to be paying much attention to the rest but was polishing his too-long nails on his silk handkerchief and eyeing with marked disfavor his neighbor, a roughly dressed fellow whose ragged mustache was lifted now and then in an unpleasant sneer.

"Our friend of the mustache," thought Michael Karl, "doesn't seem at home with the rest of the bunch. He looks as though he thought they were a bunch of weak-minded children. I bet he's for action and the rest are holding back."

On the left of the mustached one a tiny figure, so wrapped in a crimson cloak as to be almost invisible, was huddled back in the chair, the long white fingers of one hand playing nervously with a silver chain from which dangled a cross. So the Count had one of the Church to give him council.

The Churchman's neighbor was leaning forward, paying strict attention to something the Count was saying. He had the strength of the soldier and the impatience of the mustached one, but somehow he was different. Michael Karl felt that he was out of place in that assembly. The man's black hair hung untidily over his high tanned forehead, and his mouth was eager. As he listened he agreed or disagreed with violent shakes of his head.

The man beside him was as bored as his neighbor was interested. Like the youth on the other side of the table he was in uniform although this was as drab as the boy's was bright. He was gazing over the heads of all of them humming a little tune. Like the earnest man he was out of place, his face was neither crafty, cruel nor stupid.

Michael Karl wished that he knew who they all were. He began to believe that he had stumbled upon a meeting of the Council of Nobles. Although he strained his ears he could hear only a word now and then until the Count raised his voice and their disputing voices followed.

"It is madness," said the Count dryly. "We dare not move until we have an heir for the throne."

The young man looked up from his brilliant nails. "Do I not stand next to the throne?" he asked coolly.

He with the mustache favored the boy with a look of great contempt. "The people can stand much, but they will refuse to stomach you, Marquisa."

The Marquisa shot him such a glance of pure hatred that even the mustached one appeared a little uneasy.

The Count was speaking again. "Herr Kamp is right. We can not bring any other than a Karloff to the throne no matter how good his claims may be."

"What is the latest news from the mountains?" demanded the soldier.

The Count answered wearily. "The usual thing, which is nothing. The boy was probably killed long ago. He had no chance in the Werewolf's hands."

"Then," said General Oberdamnn heavily, "we are finished."

"I think," it was the man in the dull uniform who broke the silence, "that I may now have the pleasure of saying 'I told you so.' You should have kept Urlich Karl."

"Nonsense!" exploded the youth in green.

The man leaned across the table. "How much did you get out of the Laubcrantz mines, Marquisa? And why did you spend a certain week-end in the mountains?"

The Marquisa jumped to his feet. He was very pale, and Michael Karl watched his hand clench as if to strike the speaker.

"Gentlemen, gentlemen," chided the Count.

The man paid no attention to him. "The time has come," he spoke slowly, "for a little plain speaking, if," he paused and looked about him, "if there can be such a thing here. You want the money the American company can pay for the concession of the sulphur mines. That was and is the whole root of this cursed business. Well, because you knew that Urlich Karl wouldn't allow the wealth of the country to become the property of foreigners, because you knew that he would never sign the concession papers, Urlich Karl disappeared, and the Council according to law was proclaimed regent. And then you discovered that only the king may sign concessions. Count Kafner produced the American Prince and lost him to the Werewolf. Now, gentlemen, we are right where we were before. Who is going to sign that concession and make it legal?

"I promised to support your pretender with the weight of my influence because there were no more Karloffs left in Morvania. And while I live," he stared straight at the Marquisa, "there shall be none but a Karloff on the throne of Morvania. My line has certain old loyalties which can not be broken even by such as I. But lately I have heard things. Count Kafner, did you or did you not order the death of Urlich Karl?"

General Oberdamnn's face was almost purple, and the man with black hair was tearing a sheet of paper before him into bits with a rasping sound. The youth flicked his tongue in and out like a lizard he so resembled. While the sneer of the man with the mustache was more pronounced, and even the Churchman shifted in his chair.

"Did you?" asked the man again. Only the soldier remained unmoved.

The Count seemed to be making a decision. At last he spoke. "I did," he answered frankness with frankness; "it seemed best at the time. The Prince had certain ideas which were a menace to our plans. But"—he paused—"my orders were not carried out. There was some one before us."

"Who?"

"The Werewolf. The Prince was stopped that night before he reached my men."

The man in the dull uniform leaned back in his chair. "At least you can tell the truth when you wish, my dear Count. So the Werewolf has deprived us of two Princes? Well, and what are you going to do about the American concession now? Again I warn you that you can't put it through without the King's signature. And I swear to you," his voice rang very clear, "I swear to you that the Marquisa Cobentz will never mount the throne while any of my name live. You might as well turn the country over to the Communists and be done with it.''

The Marquisa was leaning over, staring straight into the man's face. "Don't swear, Duke Johann, oaths that you can not keep.''

Duke Johann smiled sweetly. "Where I go, Laub, Karnow, Kallhant, Conve and Kaptan will follow with everything they possess. The entire nobility except your bootlickers will take their cue from me.''

"Not," the Marquisa grinned like a wolf, "not if they believe you're one of the murderers of Urlich Karl.''

Duke Johann showed no surprise. "I expected that. You can not do it.''

"Rumor is an ugly thing, and if you were to vanish for a day or two, who would there be to stop men talking?''

"I!" the black-haired man almost shouted. "I want to free the people of Morvania, but I'm not going to use lies, trickery or murder. If anything happens to the Duke, the *Nationalist* and all the rest of my papers will print the whole story of what has gone on in this room. No matter what happens to me, that story will go to press if I don't report in person to my office every morning. And, Marquisa, the whole episode of the Laubcrantz Mines is part of that story.''

The Marquisa turned pasty white and sank into his chair. Duke Johann smiled at the man by his side. "Bravo, Lukrantz! Had we but one of the Karloffs to lead us, we could pull out of this mess after all.''

One of the Karloffs! Michael Karl straining to

catch every word stared down at the Duke. One of the Karloffs. He was one, he had only to step out and the Duke would make him king. While he hesitated, playing with the thought, the Count spoke again.

"We have a month to clear and then we must go."

Duke Johann stared at him, and when he spoke there was such contempt in his voice that the Count started as if he had been cut with a whip. "So the rats are thinking of leaving. Well, I and mine stay."

The man with the mustache leaned forward. "You and yours, my fine duke? Well, I and mine will make an end of all of you. We've had enough of the nobles and their doings. It is about time the South had a little to say in the government. The day of the Karloff and his lily-livered flunkies is over. The people are going to rule."

The Duke surveyed him as if he were some sort of a strange animal.

"So the people wish to rule," he said gently. "Well, perhaps they won't make as big a mess as we have; but to reach the throne they will have to climb a wall, Friend Kamp, a wall I think they won't attempt just yet. Do you know what that wall is?"

Kamp growled some sort of an answer.

"That wall," the Duke went on, his voice a smooth and deadly purr, "is composed of the bodies of every noble and every loyal man in the kingdom. We all remember Russia, Kamp, where I believe you did business, and forewarned is forearmed. You will find us ready."

Kamp sneered. "That is as it is. You will see the Red Flag on the Fortress yet."

"It grows late," said the Count hurriedly.

Duke Johann, Lukrantz and Kamp took the hint. Kamp hurried away with the briefest of good nights while the Duke and Lukrantz followed more leisurely. The Marquisa stamped out by himself frowning horribly, and the little man in the red robe scuttled behind him still holding his silver cross.

Michael Karl was about to ease his aching feet by dropping down when he saw that the three men left were not going to leave at all. They got up from the table, to be sure, but instead of going to the door they were crossing the room to a point directly below Michael Karl. He realized that the secret door was more than a foot above the floor.

He could no longer see them through the peephole but he could still hear them. There was the sound of an opening drawer and then the soldier spoke.

"Duke Johann may control the nobility, but, what Kamp says is true, the day of the nobility is over. The Duke is getting out of hand. He should be reasoned with," he ended with a dry unpleasant laugh.

Some one drew in his breath with a sharp whistling sound.

"Then you think that Kamp is the man to bargain with?" demanded General Oberdamnn.

"Nobody could bargain with Kamp, he actually believes the stuff he preaches. No, he wouldn't save our sinking ship if we gave him the key to the treasury." That was the soldier again.

"Then what can we do, Laupt?" wailed the General. "We have no Prince to produce, and the Council has their accounting next—"

"If you are worrying about those military funds you, shall I say, borrowed, you needn't be afraid. Your share of the concession will pay it up." Again the soldier laughed unpleasantly.

"But you heard what the Duke said: the concession has to be signed by the king and there is no king."

"The Marquisa is next heir to the throne, General."

"But, Major Laupt," broke in the Count, "no one would support his claim."

"No?"

"You have a plan?" asked the General eagerly.

"Perhaps. Is there any way we can trick the Duke out of Rein for the next week or so?"

"We might," the Count said slowly, "suggest that new information has been received which leads us to believe that Urlich Karl is a prisoner and we know the place where he is imprisoned. All the information coming from a loyal spy. It is a thin story, but it may do and get the Duke and all his crew out. For if Johann believed that Urlich Karl was still alive, he would storm the gates of Hell for him and every one of the nobles would cheerfully aid him in doing it."

"Then we must fix up our story to-night. General Oberdamnn, you are chief of the secret service. Who is on duty in the mountains now?"

"No one. Our last spy," the General's voice shook a little, "came floating down the Laub with his throat cut."

"Well, who might be there?"

"Dimk might. He has some reputation too."

"Where is he now?"

"Off on one of those silent hunts of his. He works without orders but he usually brings in just what we want although sometimes he doesn't report for days at a time."

"Would Johann believe Dimk?"

"Yes, Dimk worked under Johann once."

"That is excellent. Then this is what we'll do."

Michael Karl found that he could hear better by crouching down in the passage and putting his ear against the door.

"To-morrow"—began the Major.

Chapter VIII

Michael Karl Hears What Was Not Meant
For His Ears

"To-morrow," said Major Laupt, "Dimk will come to you with a story. You will of course be alone when he comes. Urlich Karl was not killed a year ago but is being held prisoner by the Were-wolf in the Laub Mountains"—the Major broke off with a laugh. "It has just occurred to me that the Werewolf might finish off Johann and his men and thank us for sending him the chance if the Duke goes too deeply into the mountains. Well, Johann's Prince will be there waiting for him."

"But we'll have to have some proof, we can't produce Dimk. Why, I don't even know where the man is," protested the General.

"You will have proof. The estate of the late Crown Prince contains a ruined mountain castle which no one but the wolves or a forester has visited these last ten years. In fact most people have forgotten about it. What more probable than that the Werewolf has made it his headquarters— it is in the heart of his country—and is holding the Prince a captive there? I can furnish you a map of the castle and the surrounding country."

"But," protested the General again, "Johann will demand to see Dimk and question him himself. Johann is no fool."

"That, of course, is the weak spot," admitted the Major. "But we must be firm upon the point that Dimk has returned to watch the Prince and his captor."

"Will Johann believe any story that we tell? He knows we hated Urlich Karl," the Count was doubtful now.

"He knows that we must have a prince to save ourselves from the public accounting. Perhaps you can suggest delicately, my dear General, that the Prince has remained where he is through our efforts. Johann would be apt to believe that. That would help the Dimk part too. Or better yet, you play the craven, Oberdamnn; go to Johann secretly and reveal this plot of ours and tell him all about the Prince. Pretend that you're afraid of Kamp and his supporters."

"I'll try," promised the General with no great relish.

"You'll do better than try, Oberdamnn," snapped the Count.

"To-night, within the hour, you will pay a visit to Kamp," continued the Major. "You will tell him that Count Kafner wishes to see him at ten tomorrow morning. From Kamp's lodgings you will go straight to the Pala Horn and demand to see the Duke. They will tell you that he isn't in, he's attending some sort of a meeting at the Journalist's Club with Lukrantz. You will seem much disturbed. Mutter a little and pace the floor, do

anything to impress upon the minds of the
servants that you are deeply worried about something, but be sure and come away before twelve
when the Duke will arrive. Tell the butler that you
will call his master in the morning as you can no
longer wait. And call upon him as early as you can
within reason. Remember you've got to act your
part well. You must give Johann the impression
that you have cold feet about this whole affair and
are ready to talk. Give him something to think
about."

"With Johann out of the city"—suggested the
Count.

"With Johann out of the city we begin to work.
Lukrantz must be muzzled, I leave that to you.
Kamp will be told that we are ready to see things
his way if he will support Cobentz for king. He will
agree because he will think he sees a chance of
raising the people against us, Cobentz being what
he is. Yes, Kamp will join us with his tongue in his
cheek."

"Next Sunday the Archbishop must preach a
very moving sermon, we'll get Mantz to write it, all
about the ancient Karloffs, and at the end he will
pray for Michael Karl as one dead. That will set
the people to thinking. Then we produce a body
and hold a state funeral. Cobentz must make a
parade of great sorrow as chief mourner. That will
identify him with the throne in the eyes of the
people."

"But the people hate Cobentz," protested the
General.

"Just so. That's where Kamp comes in. He will
try to organize a revolution, and so will we. Kamp

will raise the red flag and we the silver standard"—

"For Cobentz?"

"No, you fool, Cobentz will be disposed of, only Kamp will believe that he is our man. We will raise it for the Duke; he has Karloff blood and the nobles will follow him."

"He'll never accept the throne."

"But, my dear Count, he will not be here to refuse, and our cry of the Duke for king will confuse the issue until we're safely out of the whole muddle. I, for one, find Morvania too confining anyhow. And I believe you gentlemen will be ready to follow me over the border. We can fill our pockets at the Treasury before we go."

"But what will happen in the end?" asked the General.

"What do we care? We've made our pile and will be safely out of it. Do you agree to the plan?"

"Of course, of course," they hastened to assure the Major.

"Then it's time for you to be off, General. Remember, Kamp first and then the Pala Horn. I wish you a very good night, gentlemen."

They moved away and Michael Karl could no longer hear their voices. So they were going to start a revolution and a counter-revolution and then leave Morvania to her fate were they? Well, Michael Karl had a word or two to say on that subject. No wonder the Werewolf was so dead against the rulers. Now if the Werewolf and a choice assortment of his pack could be turned loose on Kamp and the rest of his ilk with special attention to Major Laupt—Michael Karl drew in his breath sharply. The Werewolf against the Council, the Werewolf to win! That was an idea.

Johann must be warned of course. He and Lukrantz might do something to stem the tide. And Michael Karl must get word to both of them. He arose stiffly from his aching knees and almost ran down the passage and the steps. Dropping his torch on the ledge he jammed down the lever viciously. The panel swung outward and he almost fell into the room.

"John!"

Michael Karl, dazed by the light, stared straight into the face of the American.

"Yes," Michael Karl leaned against the desk, breathing heavily from his run, "I know the secret. Tell me, how do I reach the house of Duke Johann?"

"And what do you want with Duke Johann, boy?" From behind Ericson arose the bored gentleman in the drab uniform whom Michael Karl had seen at the Council table a short hour before.

"I want to tell you not to believe Oberdamnn," said Michael Karl. He was no longer to be surprised at anything. Somehow it seemed very natural that the Duke should have been there very much at home and smoking one of the American's long cigarettes.

"Perhaps," suggested the Duke pushing forward a chair, "you had better sit down and tell us the whole story."

He was in command now, and Ericson was back in the shadow where Michael Karl couldn't see his face.

So Michael Karl told the whole story, the discovery of the passage by chance, the loss of the letter (he produced and laid it on the desk before the American), his second trip, and what he had overheard in the council chamber. They were very quiet when he had finished. The Duke was leaning back in his chair, blowing one perfect smoke ring after another while Ericson had shaded his eyes with his hand.

"So Oberdamnn is the bait and Laupt the trap. Well, well," remarked the Duke, "the passage has served us well after all. And who may you be?" He turned to Michael Karl.

In answer Michael Karl pulled the diamond Cross from beneath his shirt. "I thought once that I had some small right to wear this."

The Duke's eyebrows were raised very high. "So you are the pretender?"

Michael Karl nodded. "I never wanted to rule," he said as if to himself.

"You won't have to," the Duke assured him. "Laupt has a good story, and the queer thing about it is that it is true. Urlich Karl is still alive."

Ericson made a swift movement with his hand, and the Duke stopped.

"I think," said the American abruptly, "that enough has been said. Here," he pulled a small black book from the drawer before him and pushed it across the desk towards Michael Karl, "is your passport. The sooner you leave Morvania the better for all concerned. There is money for your passage inside that."

Michael Karl fingered the book. "Then," he said very slowly, "you wish to get rid of me?"

"In your own words," returned the American coldly, "you wish to be free of Morvania. It is better that you go now. You have done us a great service for which we thank you."

Michael Karl picked up the passport and opened it. He returned to the desk top the thick wad of paper gruden which was inside. The American wanted him out of it. That hurt.

"Thank you for the passport," he was looking down for he was afraid of what he might do if he saw the American's face. "I do not need the money. This also belongs to some one else." He unhooked the Cross and laid it beside the money. "You will give all the thanks I want if you will return it to the owner. The curse is working, it seems."

He stuffed the passport into his hip pocket and started for the door, only to turn again just before he went out. "The Werewolf might be of more help than you think," he suggested.

So the American was through with him. Well, he couldn't expect much else after what had happened to the letter and the secret passage. There was really nothing he had to pack, but he had better get his tunic, it was cold walking. And since he had refused the American's money, he would have to leave Morvania on his own two feet. He mounted the stairs.

This then was where adventuring got you. You might save a kingdom, but you lost your best friend. He wondered what Urlich Karl was like and wished a bit wistfully that he might have seen his cousin. His tunic was on the chair.

Something in an inner pocket rustled when he

picked the coat up. His investigating fingers found a scrap of paper. It was a sketch the American had once made of him in the armor of a knight. He had laughingly assured Michael Karl that he looked just like one of the crusading Karloffs and had proved his point by sketching the picture from memory with Michael Karl's face above the breast-plate. Michael Karl folded it carefully and tucked it away again.

"Michael Karl."

Michael Karl started. By the door of his room the American stood very tall and straight.

"Where are you going?"

Michael Karl shrugged. "America, of course. I came from there."

"Why won't you take that money?"

"Really, you know, I am not used to being paid to get out when I'm not wanted."

"Do you believe that?"

Michael Karl didn't answer. He wished that the American would get away from the door so he could get out.

"You know you don't believe that." This time it was a statement instead of a question.

Michael Karl refused to look at him. He turned and was staring out of the window at the domed roof of the Cathedral.

"You know that I want you, but not against your will. I guessed your name and rank from the first and, well, you see you wouldn't trust me, and I have a devil of a temper. I didn't mean what I said downstairs. We do need you badly."

Michael Karl refused to believe. There was the matter of the secret passage.

As if reading his thoughts the American continued, "That was the best thing that ever happened to our cause, when you found the passage and stumbled on the meeting. Will you stay? We haven't much to offer," the American laughed shortly, "and the whole wild thing may end with us blindfolded before a firing squad, but it will be fun while it lasts. I suppose that I shouldn't urge you into it"—

Michael Karl turned on him. "Of course I'm in it. I've been in from the first and loved every minute of it, although I didn't realize it until just now. And," he added eagerly, "I really can obey orders."

The American laughed. "I shall believe that miracle when I see it. Now come down and join us. The Duke is very much interested in you. And we have another gentleman coming to see us, a Herr Lukrantz."

"He's the newspaper man," nodded Michael Karl.

The American stared at him in surprise. "Is there anything you don't know?" he asked.

Michael Karl nodded. "Where is Urlich Karl?"

"That," said Ericson as they went down the stairs, "is just what we would all like to know.

"The Council's men did not get him. It appears they blame the whole business on the Werewolf. They don't stop to consider," he spoke very slowly emphasizing every word, "that the Werewolf never appeared until a month after Urlich Karl vanished."

"But the Werewolf himself told me"—protested Michael Karl.

"What? That Urlich Karl was murdered in a private quarrel, and he only hinted at that if I remember rightly what you told me. It looks very much as if the Werewolf wants Urlich Karl dead just as badly as we want him alive."

"Quite right." The Duke was standing before the fire waiting for them. "The Werewolf wants him dead. Does that suggest anything to Your Highness?"

Michael Karl's only idea seemed too wild to tell. "Perhaps"—he ventured—"perhaps there is some connection between the Werewolf and the Prince."

Duke Johann smiled, and the American laughed. "You guessed what it took Johann months to discover. The Werewolf either is Urlich Karl or some one very near to him. He got into communication with our party for the first time a month ago."

"Those were the mysterious green letters," explained the American.

"You say that Kafner and Laupt want me out of Rein for the week?" asked the Duke.

Michael Karl nodded.

"Then I'll go, quite publicly, so that a great crowd can testify to my going. Can you spare me a bed and a place at your table for the rest of the week?" He turned to the American.

"Gladly," Ericson answered. "You can use the secret passage too, no extra charge."

The Duke arose lazily. "That last is too tempting. I accept. You may expect a mysterious visitor soon after nightfall to-morrow. And now I must take my leave. Tell Lukrantz, when he comes, that the papers he wants concerning Cobentz's latest activities are waiting for his messenger in the usual place. I am glad," he smiled at Michael Karl, "that Your Highness had been persuaded to join us. And now, gentlemen, good-night. If you should happen to look about nine to-morrow you will see me departing for the mountains. I can assure you that my exit will be worth watching."

"We'll be standing behind the curtains in the drawing room," Ericson assured him.

The Duke laughed and left them.

"There," said Ericson, "goes the brains of the Royalist Party in Rein. He has played the hardest sort of a double game for the last nine months. There hasn't been a minute of the day or night that he hasn't been ready to feel the prick of a dagger between his shoulders. And yet, to hear him talk, you would believe that all of this has been the most amusing sort of sport."

"I like him," said Michael Karl impulsively.

Ericson nodded. "The only people who don't are a few worthies whom you saw this evening. That Council, with the exception of Lukrantz and Johann, is a gathering of the biggest bunch of crooks in the country.

"Oberdamnn is just an inefficient bungler who uses his position for what he can get out of it and who is afraid of his own shadow. Kafner wants power. He would be perfectly happy as a prime minister under some figurehead king. Laupt is just plain wolf and the nastiest one of the crowd.

"The Archbishop is pretty old, and I don't think he knows what it's all about even yet. They promised him some lands which the Church and the State have been quarreling over for the past two centuries, so he's satisfied.

"Kamp wants revolution, the bloodier the better. In his dreams he sees himself a sort of Morvanian Lenin. Though the truth about Kamp is that he really believes the stuff he preaches and that makes him dangerous.

"Then we come to Cobentz. He is an example of everything a nobleman should not be. There are some very black stories about him, and we have proof that more than half of them are true. He made a fortune out of the Laubcrantz sulphur mines, but I should hate to have to tell how he mistreated his slavelike working people to do it. His own class will have nothing to do with him with the exception of one or two petty nobles of his own sort. The throne is his goal, of course. He has Karloff blood. And he's as dangerous as a cornered rat because he never fights in the open. His enemies are apt to be found in some dark street with a dagger between their shoulders or just disappear altogether."

Michael Karl was remembering something, something which the Werewolf had flung at him as a taunt. "Did Cobentz ever have anything to do with a building called the 'Lion Tower'?" he asked.

The American jumped to his feet, and strode down the room. When he returned to answer, his voice was curiously muffled.

"The Lion Tower is his military command, and as long as the Council is ruling he has full power there. What goes on behind its walls is one of the many things he will answer for some day. What do you know of the Lion Tower?"

"When the Werewolf was questioning me, he accused me of being responsible for something which happened there," explained Michael Karl.

"The taking of that tower is Johann's job. Whatever secrets it conceals will be known then. But I think that the Werewolf will enjoy meeting Cobentz if he gets the chance," said the American softly. "And let us hope he gets it soon."

There was a timid rap at the great doors, and at Ericson's loud "Come in," Jan sidled around.

"Dominde, the Dominde Lukrantz is here."

"Show him in," the American commanded in a voice which sent the little man almost running from the room.

Lukrantz bustled in. His hair was just as ruffled and his eyes were blazing just as they had been in the Council Chamber. He carried a fat brief-case which he dropped on the nearest chair as he entered.

"Good evening," he nodded towards them both.

"Sit down, Herr Lukrantz. We are both more than glad to see you. This is High Highness, Prince Michael Karl."

Even Ericson had to laugh at the open-mouthed wonder of the man.

"Yes, it's perfectly true," he said answering the bewildered look Lukrantz gave him. "His Highness is one of us. Now doesn't that sound just like a secret society of bomb throwers? We should all be wearing beards or black masks. Yes, His Highness is one of us and he brought us some very interesting news this evening. You may tell your story again, boy."

Thus encouraged, Michael Karl told the story of the secret passage and what he had overheard there for the second time that evening.

"Watch out, Lukrantz, they're after your hide now," said the American when he had finished. "Johann is going to fall in with their plans. He is leaving the city to-morrow."

"But—" Lukrantz had begun to protest.

"He is coming back again," Ericson interrupted to reassure him. "In fact I believe that if you visited us to-morrow evening you would find him sitting right here. It is you we will have to watch out for."

Lukrantz smiled grimly. "I'm taking every precaution I can until after the sixteenth." He turned to Ericson with pathetic eagerness, "You are sure Urlich Karl will strike then?"

"He has given his word. Unless something happens to hasten matters, you may print the proclamation I gave you on the morning of the sixteenth. And by nightfall Rein will be Urlich Karl's."

Lukrantz sighed. "It is almost too much to hope for. And now to business. I have those plans you wanted of the mountain forts."

He reached for his brief-case and ruffled through the many papers it contained until he found two flimsy slips covered with meaningless wiggly lines.

"Good!" applauded Ericson. "And with some information I got this morning"— He turned to Michael Karl. "Will you please get the horse trader's letter and that map of the northern pass which came in this morning. And with this information," he continued, "our success in this part of the country is assured. I shall send it on to-night."

Lukrantz eyed the steel files almost with awe. "There is more material in there about Morvania than was ever gathered together by any one man before. The thing's a treasure chest."

"That is the advantage of being a prospective author. The cabinet stays there day in and day out, dusted by a housemaid every morning, and no one would believe me if I told them that there is information in there which would wipe a kingdom off the map.

"And now," he spread the papers Michael Karl had handed him out on his desk, "let's see what our allies over the mountains will need."

Chapter IX

In Which Two Plot And One Acts

Michael Karl missed Duke Johann's grand exit the next morning for the simple reason that he overslept. So if Ericson watched from behind the drawing-room curtain he watched alone, but Michael Karl had cause to believe that the American was far from the drawing-room curtains at the moment when the Duke's car purred down the Pala Horn.

When he as last dashed guiltily down the stairs, Michael Karl found the dining room empty and the table cleared, but for a note addressed to him in the American's sprawling hand.

I am sorry I can't be there to see Johann make his exit [he read], but I have gone to beard a certain wolf in his den. Should you have cause to reach me suddenly, send a messenger to the flower market on the bridge. At the far end is a lame man selling shrubs. The messenger is to ask for yellow roses, and the man will reply that he has none. Then the messenger will say: "Yellow roses need the sun." The answer will be: "The sun rises on the sixteenth." Simple, isn't it, and quite melodramatic. But you see, Michael Karl, you quite stepped out of modern life when you chose to complicate matters by becoming a pretender to the throne in Morvania. And I think that the above ritual matches well with secret passages and werewolves. Don't you agree with me?

And now I really must be off. If you find time too heavy on your hands, you may amuse yourself copying the material in the second drawer of the library desk. Console Johann for my absence and leave everything to him. Shall I give your regards to the Werewolf?

Yours in haste,
F.E.

Michael Karl memorized the formula of the sun and the yellow roses while he finished his lonely breakfast. He rather wistfully wondered what Ericson was doing in the mountains as he went into the library to busy himself with the contents of the second drawer.

But work could no longer hold his interest with the panel of the secret passage before him, and a calendar on the desk shrieking the fact that this was the fourteenth and that the all important sixteenth was but two days away. Half-heartedly he attempted to copy one of the papers but, after spoiling three sheets and tearing the fourth badly when he pulled it out of the typewriter, he gave it up as a bad job and went to look out of the window which fronted a short street running into the Pala Horn.

Rein was very quiet that morning. Even the sellers of fruit and flowers who fearlessly invaded the Pala Horn shouting their wares were now nowhere to be seen. Michael Karl, thinking of the brew which he had been preparing the night before, didn't like that quiet. It savored too much of a lull before the storm.

For the first time since his coming to Rein he wanted to be out. He wanted to see the Cathedral Square, the markets, to walk the dark alleys of the Bargo, to be doing something. Ericson was off to see that strange ally and perhaps Prince, the Werewolf; Johann was busy pulling wool over the eyes of the Council, Lukrantz had his part to play with his newspapers, but Michael Karl had to sit and wait. And he began to realize that that was the hardest part of all.

The two hours that followed were the dullest that Michael Karl had ever known. He tried his copying again, he made a restless tour of the downstairs rooms, he even picked up his language studies, but nothing held his interest. The panel fascinated him and he was tempted to try it, but it refused to yield to his fingers and he guessed shrewdly that the American had locked it in some way to keep him out of mischief.

He was staring out of the window for the tenth time when Jan came fluttering in, his pudgy hands shaking in distress, with a wild-haired Lukrantz at his heels.

"Where is he?" demanded the editor.

"He's gone to meet the Werewolf," answered Michael Karl, rightly thinking that Lukrantz meant the American.

"That is bad, bad." The editor sank into a chair and looked up at Michael Karl with real distress in his face. "We must get word to him. Kellermann, whom we have depended upon, has betrayed the plan for the sixteenth. If we can't reach the mountain men we are finished."

"It looks," Michael Karl pulled open the upper desk drawer and took out the snub-nosed revolver which he had always seen there, "as if I'm going to want some yellow roses after all."

Lukrantz sat and stared at him a bit stupidly.

"What do you want to tell Ericson?" asked Michael Karl as he loaded the revolver from a box of cartridges and filled his breeches pocket with the remainder.

"Just that Kellermann has betrayed us and that we need instructions. I wish Johann were here"—

"Speak of the devil," announced a cool voice from the doorway. The tall Duke, lazy as ever, stood there.

Lukrantz was out of his chair and at the Duke's side in an instant. "Kellermann" — he began shrilly.

"Has gone over to Laupt," finished the Duke for him. "Oh, yes, I heard all about it, and as there was no further use in my leaving the city to please Kafner I came back. And where are you going, Your Highness?" he asked sharply as Michael Karl started out of the door.

"To warn Ericson," answered Michael Karl mistrusting the look the Duke gave him.

"I'm sorry, Your Highness, but I must insist that you are too valuable to play the role of messenger boy. We have several who can do that very nicely."

"But I am going to do it." Michael Karl didn't say that aloud. He had an idea that Prince or no Prince that was not the sort of thing he would care to say to the Duke. After all there was no use quarreling over the fact that he was going. Let them think that he had given up and was being a nice obedient boy.

With reluctance he answered, "All right. I am ready to do anything you wish me to."

"It is most kind of Your Highness to accept matters in this manner. Though," the Duke smiled, "from what I have heard you are not always so amiable. And now if you will excuse us, Your Highness. Lukrantz, the plans for the North"—

Johann led the editor towards the desk, and their voices trailed off into half whispers. Michael Karl stiffened. Treat him like a baby would they? Well!

He tiptoed upstairs and raided the American's room for a certain black leather coat. For May the mountains would be very cold. He transferred the loose shells into one of the large patch pockets on the coat and crammed his peaked chauffeur's cap into the other.

The library door was closed when he came downstairs, but some one spoke quite loudly as he passed it.

"Of course, he will try it, Lukrantz, but Benner is outside, and he won't get far."

Michael Karl gave the door a low bow. "Thank

you, Your Grace," he said softly, "I know now how not to go."

He turned aside and pushed through the door which led to the service quarters. As he went down a narrow hall past a half-open door he caught a glimpse of Breck, his magnificent livery coat laid aside, polishing knives like any other lowly mortal while Jan was restlessly passing to and fro frowning over a printed list in his hand.

Certain tempting smells betrayed the kitchen, and a dampish, sudsy odor of the laundry. This was his chance. The laundry gave upon a square side yard where, upon the occasion, he had seen a thin sharp-faced woman wrestling with wet sheets and a slack line.

Michael Karl tried the door, and it swung open easily beneath his touch. The room was dimly lighted, and the outer door he was searching for stood ajar upon the stone paved court. He stopped to pull on the cap and fold the coat over his arm hoping to give a good imitation of a chauffeur on important business.

The stone-paved yard had a blue, painted door leading into the side street. Michael Karl's heart sank as he pushed at it; the thing was locked. But as he stepped to one side to see if he could climb the wall he saw tucked between two loose bricks the missing key. It took but a second to pull it out, unlock the door, and step into the street.

He locked the door behind him and tossed the key over the wall. When they found it lying there they would think that it had fallen out of its hiding place. Michael Karl pulled the peaked cap a little over one eye so that it set at the exact rakish angle demanded by young chauffeurs, and set off briskly down the deserted street. His adventuring had begun again.

This side street led into the Pala Horn, and a block away lay the Cathedral Square. The silvery chimes in the tall bell tower marked the hour of high noon as Michael Karl crossed the square to the avenue, which, if he had remembered Ericson's directions correctly, would lead him straight to the bridge of the flower market.

He shifted the leather coat from his right to his left arm so the revolver in the inner breast pocket would stop bumping against his side. The same recklessness which had betrayed him the night he left the Royal Train was urging him on.

Rein evidently went home for its dinner. All along the streets he could see the shop assistants, the prosperous merchants and the shoppers going home. Shop after shop was closed with a neat sign, the Morvanian "Out to Lunch," he supposed, on the door.

Michael Karl walked a little faster. After all it would never do to reach the flower market and find the man with the shrubs gone.

With a sudden dip the avenue swung downwards to meet the old bridge. Like the day when he had first seen it, it was a mass of color. A whole basket of deep purple violets was framed in clumps of yellow daffodils and some pale pink rose-like flowers. The flower girls were filling their wide aprons with tight little bunches of bright green ferns and quaint nosegays of their wares to hawk in the upper market place.

Walking slowly as if inspecting each dealer's flowers Michael Karl crossed the bridge until he came at last to the place he was seeking. Prickly shrubs uprooted, even a small tree or two, whose roots were carefully wrapped in sacking, hedged in a merry fellow who had a laugh and cheery greeting for every passer-by.

A stout, flabby-faced man was pricing a small tree and looking more than annoyed at the cripple's comments, each emphasized with a prod of his rubber-tipped cane. At last the customer pulled out his purse and carefully counted some coins into the young man's hand. He picked up his little tree and marched off looking very important while the cripple limped out into the street and busied himself with rearranging the shrubs to cover the gap left by the sapling.

Michael Karl swallowed uncertainly and stepped up to him.

"What can I do for you, friend?" asked the man cheerily, looking up at Michael Karl's approach.

"Have you any yellow roses?" Michael Karl saw the man's eyes widen, and he hesitated before he answered.

"They are not common at this season of the year."

Michael Karl nodded. "It is true that yellow roses need the sun."

"But then," the man laughed gaily as if he were telling some amusing story, "the sun will rise on the sixteenth."

"Very well." Michael Karl waited. He was to obey the flower merchant's instructions, it seemed.

"A friend of mine may have some really yellow roses," began the man thoughtfully; "if you wish you might try there. Go straight ahead until you come to the sign of the Four Horses and inquire there for Franz Ultmann. Ask him for roses."

"Straight on?"

"Yes. Good hunting, friend."

"Thank you," and with a pleasant nod Michael Karl went on wondering just how large a cog in Ericson's machine was the flower merchant.

He was in the New Town now, and his way led him by the flapping Union Jack and the carved lions of the British Embassy and the cross-looking eagle and stars and stripes of its American neighbor. How long ago was it that he had claimed American citizenship? Maybe after the excitement was over he would make use of the passport which still lay in the drawer of his bedroom table.

The street curved around the river bank and he came upon what must have been, when it was built, a country inn. A sign of four wild-looking horses swung over the entrance to its courtyard which was now almost choked with a very large ox cart and a very small roadster. Close to the wall a draggled cock and two greedy hens hunted their dinner fearlessly among the hay upon which the unyoked oxen were making a meal. The sleepy dog by the door aroused himself to snap at an annoying fly as Michael Karl stepped over him.

The long low room of the inn parlor wasn't crowded. A brightly dressed farmer, the apparent owner of the ox cart, and one other customer were talking to the plump and pretty barmaid. The man at the bar turned away after a moment and smiled cheerily at Michael Karl.

"Hot, ain't it?" he asked, wiping the shining red spot above his scanty fringe of sandy hair with a handkerchief printed in a pattern of horses' heads. He was a short, stocky man and the wide riding breeches and cloth gaiters he wore made him look very wide indeed.

"It certainly is," Michael Karl agreed. The man seemed a friendly person. He stepped to the bar and spoke to the plump maid who was busily engaged in rubbing up the glasses.

"Where may I find Herr Franz Ultmann?" he inquired.

She looked at him, her eyes round with surprise. "That's him, there," she pointed with a pudgy, none too clean, finger to the man in the gaiters. "Herr Ultmann," she raised her voice to almost a shout though the man she addressed was no more than three feet away, endeavoring to light a very large and smelly pipe, "here's one that'll be a-lookin' for ye."

Michael Karl turned to Ultmann. "I've come to see about some yellow roses," he said. "The man at the flower market said you might have some early ones."

Franz Ultmann screwed up his eyes. "That I do. Will ye come and see 'em, Lad? My car be outside. And here's somethin' for that noo ribbon, m'dear." He tossed the barmaid a coin and went out into the courtyard, followed by Michael Karl.

" 'Tis funny how these yellow roses be," he said, holding open the door of the very small roadster for Michael to enter. "They need the sun. I'm told that we'll be a-havin' a very warm sun on the sixteenth. I'm head stable manager to Duke Johann, not that the Duke keeps up his stable very much since the war, but I raise my roses on the side, and a pretty thing I make out of it in a good season. But I did better in the days when the old king ruled. More goin' and comin' and the ladies bought from me. Especially yellow roses.

"D'ye ride, lad?" he interrupted himself to ask suddenly.

"Yes."

"That is good. I'll show ye a couple o' fillies that'll make ye long to get a let up on 'em. It's a pity the Duke don't care for racin' any more. In the old days his stables was one o' the sights o' the country, but now he's taken to cars like the rest o' 'em."

"Does the Duke come out often?" Michael Karl had no desire to be caught by the Duke this late in the day.

Ultmann shook his head. "No, seems like he don't care for the country no more. He's a big man in Rein since the old king died. He was sort o' out o' favor before then; supported the Prince who ran off and married a foreigner, and the king sent him off to enjoy his estates. And from what I've heard tell, the Prince that the Duke liked was the best o' the lot; he was the only one o' 'em all who dared to stand up to old Karl when he was in one o' his tantrums. A regular old pepper pot, the king was."

"Did you ever see the Prince?" asked Michael Karl. So the Duke had supported his father and had been exiled to his estates for doing so. Faith, he was learning more family history from this Ultmann than he would have ever learned from history books.

Ultmann shook his head regretfully. "I didn't come until after the king had packed him off abroad and sent all his friends, the Duke included, away from court. It was then that the Duke took to horses, and he sent to England for a man to manage his stables. That's when I came. Me father was a Morvanian what settled in England, and he was at the huntin' stables of Lord Westingham. Brought me up right, he did, an' learned me a good trade into the bargain. That's how I come here. And now, Lad, here we are."

They turned off the main road onto a narrow, hedge-bordered drive, and Ultmann got out to open the five-barred gate before them. Some horses in a neighboring field trotted up to watch them curiously. Ultmann waved his hand toward them.

"They be beauties," he said and grinned with pride when Michael Karl heartily agreed with him. "They always wants to see what a man be a-doin', bad as children, they be."

He climbed stiffly back into the car and drove through the open gate. Michael Karl volunteered to close it.

"That be right helpful of ye, Lad. I'm not so limber as I uster to be. Marthe will be right glad to see ye come in for dinner. She was remarkin' this mornin' that company was mighty few and far between for us."

Michael Karl wondered who Marthe was. "But," he said slowly, "I must see the roses."

Ultmann favored Michael Karl with a slow closing of the left eye. "The roses will keep until after dinner, Lad. I'll be a-thinkin' that ye won't find Marthe's cookin' amiss."

He steered the car around a bend in the road and into a farmyard. Some distance away from the haystack, the busy chickens and the pack of excited dogs which thrust themselves upon Ultmann, was a small, neat house with a hint of freshly laundered curtains at the windows and a budding rosebush by the door.

"The rose garden's on the other side," Ultmann informed him, "an' the stable's over there." He pointed with the stem of his stubby pipe to the long gray building a field away from them.

"An' here's Marthe, Lad."

A small woman in the neatest of print dresses stepped out of the door to welcome them.

"Franz, ye're late agin," she chided the man softly as he came up the paved walk.

"I had reason, m'dear. This lad has come about some yellow roses an' he'd like some dinner too, I'll be a-thinkin'. Such dinners as ye have, Marthe, are treats such as even the old king never got in his life."

The little lady dimpled and smiled at Michael Karl. "Ye'll come in an' wash, both of ye, and then maybe I'll be a-findin' somethin' in the oven for ye."

Ultmann led Michael Karl to a sunny bedroom and poured him a basin of cool water.

"The soap and towels be here, Lad." He swung open the door in the lower part of the washstand.

"Thank you." Michael Karl was already shedding his warm tunic and rolling up his shirt sleeves.

Washed and brushed as neatly as he could be

without either comb or clothes brush he walked into the tiny parlor a few minutes later to find his hostess setting the last of a mammoth array of steaming dishes on a table. She smiled as he came in.

"Franz will be here directly. It is nice of ye to visit us. So far are we from town that we have few callers. Now, Franz," she said to Ultmann as he came in, "the boy must stay with us awhile."

Ultmann shook his head. "He is a-huntin' yellow roses, Marthe," he answered simply.

Marthe looked up with real fear in her eyes. "But," she protested to Michael Karl, "ye're too young to—to—"

"Search for yellow roses?" Michael Karl supplied for her. "But then I've been hunting for them for some time. However, there are quite a few people," he thought of the Duke, "who feel the same way you do about it."

Ultmann sampled the soup before him. "Didn't I tell ye, Lad, that Marthe is the best cook in the country?"

Michael Karl looked up from his fast emptying plate. "I agree with you heartily."

But the praise failed to bring a smile to Marthe's worried face. "I don't like it," she murmured, still looking at Michael Karl.

He laughed. "I'll be back safe and sound, never fear, and the yellow roses with me, on the sixteenth."

Marthe still was doubtful, nor did her face clear when Michael Karl finished his dinner and prepared to follow his guide to the last trail of the yellow roses.

Chapter X

Into The Mountains At Once

Michael Karl gathered up his coat and discarded cap and was about to start down the walk after the now impatient Ultmann when Marthe came hurrying in to press a packet neatly done up in the cleanest of linen napkins into his hand.

"A little somethin' to eat. The mountains be cruel sometimes, Laddie. What will thy mother be a-thinkin' to let ye go?"

Michael Karl looked at her very gravely and then stooped to kiss her wrinkled hand. "Thank you very much. You see, my mother isn't here to worry any more."

He went quickly out of the door and joined Ultmann in the yard.

"We cross to the stables, Lad. It is a good thing ye can ride for I'll have to be givin' ye Lady Spitfire, and she be none too gentle with a stranger."

They tramped across the field and into the dirt lane which led to the stables. A groom was busy rubbing down a muddy horse and a boy was whistling through his teeth as he unloaded bales of straw from a farm wagon. But for these two, a sleepy black cat and a pair of uneasy but very plump pigeons, the stable yard was empty.

"Hans!" shouted Michael Karl's guide.

The groom dropped his brush and turned with a half salute to answer.

"Bring out the Lady and the light huntin' saddle. This young man be of a mind to try her."

The groom led his horse into an empty stall and disappeared. In a minute or two he was back leading a dainty black mare who picked her way disdainfully with her small hooves and sneered at the groom by her head.

"Here she be, Herr Ultmann. Is the young Dominde wishful for to try her on the round track?"

Ultmann shook his head. "No. He will be a-takin' her for the afternoon. He comes with orders from His Grace. Now, then, saddle her, Hans."

He followed Hans into the saddle room while the boy with the straw bales held the Lady. When he returned, he had a pair of small saddle bags over his arm.

"Will ye be so kind as to drop these at the head shepherd's hut, Lad? The mountain trail leads by it."

"Of course," Michael Karl answered as he mounted.

The Lady was inclined to be skittish, and Michael Karl found that he needed a steady hand to bring her down to business.

"Follow the path through the orchard," Ultmann said, "and when ye're through the pass give the mare her head. Good-by and good luck to ye, Lad."

"Good-by!" shouted Michael Karl over his shoulder. He could hold the dancing Lady no longer and they were off down the orchard path.

A regular shower of fragrant petals rained down upon them to tangle in the mare's short mane and powder Michael Karl's shoulders. The heavy, sweet scent of plum blossoms years after could always make him see again the dancing mare and the dirt track winding among the flowering trees. There was at least a mile of the orchard road and the mare settled down to a steady trot.

Michael Karl pulled the leather coat more comfortably across the saddle horn so that the pistol pocket lay on top. The saddle bags seemed empty and he guessed that they were to be his passport to some guardian of the hill ways.

A gate gaped before them, and they were out on a stony track which stumbled its way into a wood and so up the mountain side. The mare picked her path as daintily as a cat on a wet day and seemed to know her way. They entered the wood, and Michael Karl was grateful for the shade. The afternoon sun was decidedly warm on his shoulders.

The wood was so still about him that he dared to whistle a song that he had heard a street musician play a day or two before. It had been just at twilight, and he had shared the upper balcony with Ericson when the man had come wandering along playing the violin and singing softly.

"Listen," Ericson had gripped his arm, "he's singing one of the mountain songs which you rarely hear nowadays."

The lilting air was very sweet and they had both tossed him coins as he had passed beneath them.

And now Michael Karl tried to remember the notes.

Gradually the forest thinned out, and the trees became shrubs, the shrubs pasture land. Here and there a newly clipped sheep, its pink skin still shining through the scanty, dirty wool, stared stupidly after them or went on grazing. A wary, tangle-coated dog barked at Michael Karl sharply from the top of a rock where he had established his lookout over his master's flock.

As if the dog's bark had summoned him, a gaunt man, whose shoulders bent forward under a heavy sheepskin coat, appeared around the base of the watchdog's rock and stood quietly waiting for Michael Karl to come up to him. Michael Karl unfastened the saddle bags.

"Good day," he said pleasantly. The man stared at him and then at the worn saddle bags Michael Karl was holding out to him.

He reached for them slowly. "Ye come from Ultmann," he asked rustily as if he had not had occasion to speak for a long time.

"Yes, I do," answered Michael Karl. The mare was restless, suspicious of the dog who had left his place and come down to sniff around her ankles.

"Ye go straight up to the long peak," the shepherd pointed up the mountain, "cross the pass and down, then over the river and tell the sentry 'Rein Post.'"

He nodded curtly in answer to Michael Karl's thanks and turned away, calling his curious dog sharply to heel as he disappeared behind the rock with the saddle bags over his arm.

Michael Karl dismounted; the slope was too

steep to force the mare to carry him. He hooked the reins over his arm and started to climb. It was an hour before they reached the long peak, a shaft of solid rock like a giant's needle. A faint path wound around beneath its shadow. This must be the pass, Michael Karl thought.

He stood awhile to rest. The valley of Rein, he could see the Fortress towers and the Cathedral spire easily, lay behind him and the mysterious hunting ground of the Werewolf sloped downward from his feet before him. The mare sighed and sniffed at the downward track.

Swinging into the saddle Michael Karl obeyed Ultmann's instructions and gave the mare her head. With a right good will she started downwards. Almost immediately they were swallowed up in a forest ten times as thick and wild as that on the other side of the mountain, and yet a faint track led them on. It was the faintest of trails, but Michael Karl placed his trust in the Lady's knowledge and she seemed to know her way very well. Evidently it wasn't the first time she had used the mountain path.

The shadows were growing, and here in the forest there was a chill in the air. It wasn't long before Michael Karl was glad to slip into the leather coat he had had the forethought to bring along.

The mare halted and sniffed the air and then turned aside confidently. Within the screening bush a spring bubbled cool and clear, and she buried her nose deep in the water while Michael Karl hastened to dismount and drink from his cupped hands.

He pulled a wisp of the coarse grass and rubbed down the mare's thin legs and flanks. She was content to stand for awhile, so he pulled out the napkin-wrapped lunch Marthe had given him and ate two of the thick, satisfying sandwiches. The ride over the mountain through the crisp air had whetted his appetite.

Thrusting remains of the lunch back in his pocket, he caught the reins and swung into the saddle. It must be growing late; the shadows were very deep now. They continued their way down the slope, the mare picking her way very carefully, measuring her distances as she went.

The forest was growing thinner. Once they came upon a rude stack of wood and there were scars of recent cuttings all about them. The sun shone hot in the clearings, but the mare avoided the open spaces and kept to the tangle of trees and vines.

They were on level ground at last and through the trees Michael Karl could hear the river. He halted the mare and bent over the saddle to pull up the campaign boots. It was a good thing after all that he had raided the royal wardrobe, the ford might be deep.

Out of the trees unto a sloping bank they came at last. The mare turned downstream a hundred feet or so and then walked out cautiously in the pebble-bottomed stream. Almost at once she was beyond her depth and swimming strongly with the water rippling around her powerful shoulders and lapping unpleasantly over Michael Karl's boot tops.

As suddenly as it had fallen beneath them the bottom arose again. The mare found her footing, sneezed and stepped to shore where she stopped and shook herself like a dog. Michael Karl leaned forward to turn down his boots when some one on the bank above him spoke softly.

"Good girl, Lady. Well done!"

The mare whinnied and Michael Karl looked up. A man, in the same drab uniform that the Duke had worn the night before, was looking down, but his eyes were all for the mare instead of her rider.

Then he appeared to remember that the Lady might have a rider and the rifle which hung so comfortably in the crook of his arm pointed towards Michael Karl. This then was the sentry.

"Rein Post," said Michael Karl swiftly.

"Who to?" asked the man coolly.

"I am interested in yellow roses," answered Michael Karl deliberately, "and would like to meet any one who is interested in the same thing." Great guns, he thought, that sounded just like one of those advertisements one puts in the back of magazines asking for correspondents.

"Yellow roses," the man laughed. "If you will come up here, friend, I think I can find you some one who is interested in yellow roses."

Without waiting to see if Michael Karl followed he turned away. The mare, with a little urging from her rider, scrambled up the bank and followed their guide. This bank of the river looked almost civilized. A broad road ran along it, and the gravel-filled ruts testified not only to its use, but also to the care spent in keeping it up.

The sentry swung along it easily until he came to a mammoth oak tree where he stopped and, putting his fingers to his mouth, whistled shrilly.

Out of the bush, almost at their feet, appeared a youngster whose drab blouse was crossed by two well filled cartridge belts and who had a long-barreled rifle slung over his shoulder by a strap.

"Messenger to see *him*," the sentry indicated Michael Karl with a thrust of a dirty thumb. "Take him in."

Without another word the sentry turned back to his post by the river, and the boy came forward to take the mare's loose reins. He stared at Michael Karl curiously but did not speak.

Michael Karl longed to ask him if he were one of the wolf pack and if the American had arrived safely for his meeting with the Werewolf, who might or might not be the King of Morvania. But the guide forged straight ahead and gave him no opening. Almost unconsciously Michael Karl began to hum the mountain air which had attracted him.

The boy stopped. "Who are you?" he demanded.

Michael Karl answered with the old formula, "A seeker of yellow roses."

His questioner refused to be satisfied with that. "But that isn't their signal, that is the password of the—" Then he stopped suddenly and hurried on, deaf to Michael Karl's questions.

The road curved away from the river back into the forest, and they plodded on. Little spurts of dust arose from between the mare's hooves and the soldier's boots. Michael Karl shivered and drew the coat closer, the last warmth of the sun disappeared, and only a pale gold in the west remained. He was learning just how cool a May night in the mountains might be.

Then they came into the camp. Five tiny cabins grouped in a rough circle was the nucleus of a large city of brush huts and weather-stained tents. Before each crackled a fire fed by countless hurrying shadows. It was the camp of a large army. The Werewolf was evidently more of a power in the land than the Council guessed.

Michael Karl and his guide were noticed almost at once, and a young man in a black uniform from which all badges of rank had been removed held a whispered conversation with the soldier.

"If you will please dismount and come with me," the newcomer said at last and, as Michael Karl hesitated, added, "Reptmann will see after the horse."

Michael Karl obediently slid down from the saddle. His stiff legs moved woodenly, and he stumbled when he tried to walk. It appeared that this was the price for hours in the saddle when there were three months between this and the last ride.

He reeled in the wake of the newcomer towards the largest of the cabins. A soldier lounging near the door pulled himself up stiffly and saluted the young man smartly.

The cabin was small but it wasn't dark. Two lamps, lighted, Michael learned later, from storage batteries, stood on the table among some badly rolled maps, part of one of the huge round loaves of black bread, a bottle of the sour mountain wine and a greasy tin plate with a gnawed chicken leg on it.

A middleaged man with very tidy gray hair and a small, neatly waxed mustache was absentmindedly nibbling at a chunk of bread while he listened to a long list being read droningly aloud by a thick-lipped young man with a too-tight collar.

He looked up quickly as they entered and Michael Karl knew, by the little sigh of relief he gave, that he was very glad indeed to be interrupted.

"Well, Urich?" he asked as Michael Karl's companion saluted.

"A messenger, Colonel Haupthan."

"From whom?" The Colonel leaned forward and stared in a puzzled way at Michael Karl's face.

"Duke Johann," answered Michael Karl. Lukrantz had sent him but Johann was head of the Rein party.

"What is it?"

"I am afraid," Michael Karl said respectfully, "that I must decline to answer. I am to deliver my message directly to Mr. Ericson."

Colonel Haupthan frowned. "What do you mean? There is no Mr. Ericson with us."

Michael Karl mentally kicked himself. It was very probable that Ericson went under some other name when visiting the royal forces.

He began again. "My message is to the American who is negotiating with the Werewolf."

The Colonel arose slowly. They were all staring at him now.

"There is no American in this camp," said the Colonel.

Michael Karl's companion spoke harshly. "He claims to be one of the Yellow Roses and yet he used the signal of the Black Coats. What—"

The Colonel nodded. "I fear, my friend, that there is a great deal you must explain."

"But Ericson is here or wherever the Werewolf is. He left instructions that if anything important happened we were to reach him through the Yellow Roses."

"And I repeat that there is no Ericson among us and there never has been."

"Perhaps he calls himself something different, but he is here unless something happened to him since this morning."

"Who are you?"

Before he thought Michael Karl answered truthfully, "Michael Karl."

The Colonel sat down again. "That I know to be a lie." He picked up his bread and bit off a piece.

"Really, you know," Michael Karl answered with some dignity, "I am not used to being called a liar. And," he tried to make himself as tall as possible, "I want to see the Werewolf. You might send for him."

The Colonel looked shocked. "You will take this —this—"

"Young ruffian," Michael Karl instantly supplied for him.

"Young ruffian," obediently repeated the Colonel somewhat dazed, "and keep him under guard until His Majesty comes."

Michael Karl bowed mockingly. "Thank you so much. I trust my cell is comfortable. It is just possible that I won't need a chair; indeed, I shall probably not need one for months and months after that ride, but I do think that I deserve supper. After all, I tried to save your kingdom for you. Inform His Majesty that I'll see him at once, but then I still think that you should produce the Werewolf."

Leaving the Colonel apparently overcome by his nonsense, Michael Karl marched stiffly out to follow his soldier companion to another and much smaller hut. There was a box for a chair, another for a table and, what looked best of all, a canvas cot.

"I bag this," Michael Karl sank down on the cot. "And look here, I'm not going to play Desperate Desmond, so you needn't hang around. Just call me when you bring supper in. And while I think about it, I don't like bread and water. You may tell the Colonel so."

He buried his head in the pillow with a determined thump and closed his eyes for a moment. His jailer watched him in open-mouthed amazement and then sat down gingerly on the chair box.

Michael Karl shifted a little so he could see the top of the larger box which served as a table. There was something there which looked oddly familiar. He was right, it was the blue cover of the Kipling book, that treasure which the Werewolf had torn from him along with his cloak at their first and last interview. Then the Werewolf was here after all. What a mess if he were the King and Michael Karl's cousin.

Some one had been reading the Kipling book lately, a pinkish book mark dropped limply from between its pages. Interested and forgetting his guard, Michael Karl sat up in the cot to see the better. The book mark was a twisted silk cord with a small carved ivory ball at one end. Michael Karl whistled softly; he knew he had seen that ball before.

The American had shown it to him one day, telling him that it was a single bead and part of the cord of a Tibetan rosary. Ericson had declared that he never traveled without it, it being his lucky piece. Then this was Ericson's cabin, and the Colonel did know him.

Michael Karl lay back. He was safe, but the message he had come to deliver worried him. The guard was still sitting there on his uncomfortable box.

"I say," Michael Karl addressed him, "when is the chap who owns this cabin coming back?"

The guard looked uncomfortable. "This is my cabin," he answered shortly.

"Yes?" said Michael Karl unbelievingly. "Then what is that book doing there?" He pointed to the Kipling book.

"His Majesty," answered the guard with stiff pride, "left that there this morning."

"Well, well. That happens to belong to me." Before the guard could prevent him, he got up and reached for it.

No, he hadn't been mistaken, it was his book, and it was Ericson's charm between the pages. He opened to the pages at the back where he had kept his informal diary. Some one had been reading it and enjoying it for here and there were comments in the neatest of print.

Opposite the description of the General's table manners, the unknown had printed: "Only too true; I had to sit opposite him at maneuvers one year." Michael Karl got no farther when the book was snatched out of his hands and he looked up into the blazing eyes of the guard.

"How dare you?" demanded the young officer in a low voice.

"I'm sorry," answered Michael Karl, "but after all it is my book."

The guard made no answer, but returned to his box with the book held carefully in his hand.

Chapter XI

Michael Karl Meets His King
For The First Time

"He is in here, Your Majesty," Michael Karl heard the words, half dreaming. So the king was here at last, but really it was too much effort to open his eyes and see this cousin of his.

"Why, you lazy pup!" Some one shook Michael Karl, and he protestingly opened his eyes to see Ericson smiling down at him.

"So you're here at last," said Michael Karl plaintively, "after leaving me to the mercy of these desperados. You might have been here to meet me anyhow."

"Get up, boy, and try to show a little intelligence," said the American. "Trust you," he added feelingly as Michael Karl swung his booted feet to the floor and sat up, trying to blink the sleep out of his eyes, "to find the only comfortable cot in camp."

The room was remarkably full of strangers though there were a few old friends like the Colonel. Michael Karl wondered sleepily where the king was.

"And now perhaps you will be so kind as to tell me why you thought it necessary to join us."

"Kellermann has squealed," Michael Karl answered simply. "And now will you take your funny face away and let me sleep, please?"

"Boy," the Colonel's face was purple with wrath, "you are speaking to His Majesty!"

"Yes, you would think of court etiquette at a time like this," said Ericson wearily and dropped down beside Michael Karl.

"So Kellermann, as you say so neatly, has squealed. Well, it was my fault for trusting a man with a chin like his. Johann knows this of course?"

Michael Karl nodded, a little dazed. The Colonel said that Ericson was the king, but of course that wasn't true because the king was the Werewolf. Or was it?

"Look here," he said suddenly, "are you Urlich Karl?"

But of course he was. Beneath the light-hearted exterior of the American there had always been something which Michael Karl had felt rather than seen, a certain shy dignity and air of command. And now the American husk seemed to be crumbling away from this unknown cousin, revealing a new and rather respect-commanding person underneath.

The young man smiled in answer to Michael Karl's question. "Do you mean to say that you didn't guess it when I have given myself away so many times? Yes, I am the King, but then it doesn't look as if I am going to enjoy that title long if Laupt and his romantic friends have their way. Well, now that you are here, I suppose I shall have to put you to work. Oh, I forgot. Gentlemen, His Highness, Prince Michael Karl."

The Colonel turned a beautiful mulberry shade, and his late guard looked as if he were trying to sink through the floor. With the regularity of clockwork the room bowed and clicked. Michael Karl used the "do and die" smile which he had used with some success at the embassy presentations in the past and which he had thought to keep on ice the rest of his life.

"So Kellermann squealed," continued the King. "I like your choice of words, Michael Karl. A rat like Kellermann would squeal. Well, there's no rest for the weary it seems. Could you drag yourself over to headquarters, boy, and begin making yourself useful?"

Michael Karl got to his feet stiffly, several muscles protesting vigorously at the process. He made up his mind that he would demand the true story of the Werewolf on the first possible occasion.

"By the way did Johann send you?"

"Why, no," answered Michael Karl truthfully.

Urlich Karl sighed. "I thought," he said in a weary voice, "that you said you could obey orders."

Michael grinned impishly. "I didn't say whose orders."

His cousin stared at him. "I ought to court martial you for that you—you—"

"Young ruffian," supplied Michael Karl for the second time that evening, with his eye on the Colonel.

Urlich Karl grew very stern. "Yes, I've heard

how you deviled my officers. I don't know why you were added to the rest of my troubles. Between having you or a revolution on my hands I choose the revolution every time."

"Oh, rot!" answered Michael Karl rudely, to the consternation of the officers, and trod upon his cousin's heels as they went out the door.

The camp was alive. The fires blazed no higher before the tents, nor did there seem to be more hurrying figures in view than there had been two hours before, and yet there was an undercurrent of hurry and bustle.

Sensing Michael Karl's question Urlich Karl spoke, "We move at midnight. Luckily I thought that something like this might happen and so decided to pull out of here at midnight anyway. Kellerman can't stop us now; we'll have to take our chances."

Even as he spoke, a horse, whose sweat glistening sides were striped with foam, galloped into the square of beaten earth, and his rider, tottering with weariness, flung himself off to disappear into the large headquarters cabin.

"Something's up!" exclaimed Urlich Karl and hurried Michael Karl across.

The officers inside jumped to their feet as the royal party entered, but Urlich Karl waved them to their seats.

"Your news!" he demanded of the panting rider.

"Kafner has proclaimed Cobentz king. Innesberg has arisen. The Fortress of Rein is held by Cobentz, but the Duke holds the New Town and the Northern Pass. You must strike by midnight or he will have to fall back. All Cobentz's supplies are in the Fortress and the Reds of Innesberg are un-prepared."

"So. Well, gentlemen," Urlich Karl's voice cracked like a whip, "we cross the Northern Pass within the hour. Haupthan, you will lead the advance force out of camp in exactly ten minutes. Make for the lower pass and consolidate with what forces the Duke has left there. Cobentz and the Reds will expect us to divide and strike at both Innesberg and Rein, but to-night Rein only is our object.

"Grimvich, take the Foreign Legion through the upper pass and find the Duke. Upon his approval, go down to the old bridge, and when you get the word, sweep the Bargo. The Reds will have en-trenched themselves there and it will be dirty fighting."

A tall officer with a scarred face nodded curtly. "We will get through," he promised with sinister confidence.

"The Wolf Pack will follow me," continued the King, "and we will strike directly for the Fortress through the secret passage of the Pala Horn ac-cording to the plan we discussed last night. That leaves the Black Coats." He turned to look at Mi-chael Karl and then he hunted among the papers on the table until he found what he wanted, the Cross of Saint Sebastian.

"Remember, gentlemen, Michael Karl is the heir to the throne. The Black Coats will follow him as is their right." He slipped the silver chain over Mi-chael Karl's head so that the Royal Cross lay upon the shabby chauffeur's tunic.

"And now to work, gentlemen." And so dismissing them he was left alone with Michael Karl.

With a ghost of a smile, he faced his young cousin. "You have been raised to command as have all the Karloffs, and I shall not hamper you with orders which you have no intention of obeying, but I am going to ask you to be reasonably careful. I had hoped that you would remain with Johann in Rein until this business was over, but I am not at all surprised at your turning up. You don't have to promise a thing but if anything happens—I know you hate the thought of ruling but—"

Michael Karl looked at his tall cousin-king soberly. "If anything happens, I promise that I will do my duty."

"You will never regret that promise," answered Urlich Karl slowly. "And now for general orders. Your men are recruited from your own regiment, the Prince's Own. They are mounted rifles, crack shots. Try to take the Cathedral Square and hold it open long enough for Grimvich to get reinforcements through to me at the Fortress. I am going to use the secret passage to take a picked body of men into the Palace and try to take the Fortress. Such a sudden blow at the very heart of their defense will demoralize Cobentz's party. I am hoping that he will have withdrawn most of his men to face Johann and Grimvich in the Lower Town. Luckily Kellermann knew nothing of the passage, and they are unwarned.

"Johann will give you more definite orders when you reach him. Follow Grimvich through the higher pass, not Haupthan through the lower. Good hunting and the best of luck until I join you in the Cathedral Square. Urich!" he called, and when the officer who had been Michael Karl's guard arrived he said, "This is your commanding officer, Urich. Good luck."

Michael Karl saluted and went out. A Black Coat was holding the Lady and two other horses. Across the Lady's saddle hung a saber belt with an empty holster attached. He reached for it, buckled it on, and thrust the revolver he had brought with him into the holster.

They mounted and rode into the darkness. At the edge of the clearing was a group of mounted men whose rifles pointed skyward over their shoulders with a cocky air. Michael Karl thrilled silently. This was his first command. He had waited all his life, studied and worked all those years in America with the Colonel, for nothing else than this moment. Urich pressed a battered hunting horn into his hands.

"Our calls are sounded on this, Your Highness," explained the aide-de-camp.

"Not tonight," answered Michael Karl. "Pass the word along. We follow Colonel Grimvich."

"He has already left, Your Highness," answered a voice out of the darkness.

"Then, march!" Michael Karl gave his first command.

They swung down the military road at a slow trot. From the darkness ahead Michael Karl could hear the rattle of accouterments and a rumbling noise.

"That is the field artillery, Your Highness," said Urich in answer to Michael Karl's question.

They clattered over a wooden bridge, which the

engineers had been working on feverishly since daybreak the morning before, and in another half hour they were beginning the climb to the Pass. Above them on the mountain a fire burned ruddily as a guide.

Down the line galloped an aide.

"Colonel Haupthan's compliments, Your Highness, and do you wish to pass through his lines? The Foreign Legion is going now."

"We follow the Legion," answered Michael Karl.

Their trot lengthened into a lope, and as they passed up through the dark bulk of the artillery and the scattered clumps of infantry, the unseen men raised a faint cheer. Before them moved the Foreign Legion, their ten machine guns packed by sturdy mules used to the curving mountain paths.

At last the upward slope became so steep that they were forced to dismount and lead their horses.

"How will they get the guns up here?" demanded Michael Karl of Urich.

"The guns will take the lower pass; it is less steep but longer, Your Highness. We will be over before them."

Again the aide came back, but this time he was walking and leading his horse.

"Colonel Grimvich's compliments. He is over among Duke Johann's pickets."

"We'll join him in a minute," Michael Karl panted and they did.

On a log by an open fire lounged the Duke, as lazy as ever, with Colonel Grimvich standing near. The Duke arose languidly as Michael Karl tramped up.

"Greetings, Your Highness. So in spite of us you're at the wars?"

Michael Karl laughed somewhat nervously. He had not lost all his fear of the Duke. That gentleman had earned a great deal of his respect.

"Rein looks very peaceful, doesn't she?" the Duke went on, pointing down into the farther valley where the lights of the city strung around and around the hill like fire-flies caught in a spider's web. "Yes, it looks very peaceful from here, but there is hell brewing there.

"You will take the Legion for the bridge, Grimvich. My men held it an hour ago, but now—who knows? Anything can happen in house-to-house fighting. When you have consolidated your position, signal with the green rocket. At that His Majesty will move in through the Western Water Gate which Lukrantz and a handful of volunteers are holding open. Fifteen minutes after the flare," he turned to Michael Karl, "Your Highness will ride straight for the Cathedral Square, and nothing must stop you. The success of His Majesty's plan, his very life, depends upon keeping that square clear so that the Foreign Legion can reach him at the Fortress. This time orders must be obeyed."

He pulled back his cuff and studied the dial of his watch by the firelight.

"Quarter past three, Grimvich. Good luck."

The impassive Colonel bowed stiffly and strode away into the dark. Then from the darkness came the crunching sound of marching men, the rattle of mule harness and the whispered sound of orders. Grimvich was moving down to the bridge.

When the Foreign Legion was out of earshot, the Duke turned again to Michael Karl. "You had better move down to the outpost at the foot. Have you a watch?"

Michael Karl shook his head and the Duke unfastened the leather strap of his own. "Remember, fifteen minutes after the green rocket and don't let anything stop you."

Saluting, Michael Karl turned away to mount and, with the Black Coats behind him, he picked his way cautiously down the forest path which was so narrow that they had to go single file. A challenge in the bush stopped him at last and he found, with a sigh of relief, that he had reached the outposts.

From distant Rein the wind now and then brought the faint sound of firing. Grimvich, evidently, wasn't finding things his own way at the bridge. Michael Karl leaned forward in the saddle, straining his eyes to see, until the horn dug sharply into his ribs. His mouth was dry as he licked the dust off his cracked lips while something icy crept up and down his spine. For something to do he discarded the leather coat, hanging it carefully on a bush. After all it might be a hindrance if they came to close fighting in the narrow streets.

Longing and yet dreading to see the green flash he waited while the impatient horses stamped now and then in the bushes behind him and the men whispered.

Suddenly Urich spoke, "The dawn!"

The sky was gray in the east, but in the last few seconds of darkness a green pencil of flame rose and fell. Grimvich was through and the bridge was safely theirs. Somewhere within the city Urlich Karl was risking his life to reach the Pala Horn.

Michael Karl kept his eyes glued to the dial of the Duke's watch. It was growing lighter every second and he could see it quite easily. The hand didn't seem to move at all. Behind him he could hear the click, click of the rifles being taken off their carrying straps and loaded for action. The mare threw up her head and breathed deeply, quivering a little between his knees.

At twelve minutes Michael Karl raised his hand and Urich put the battered hunting horn to his lips. There was breathless silence behind them. The watch hand touched thirteen, fourteen, Michael Karl brought down his hand and the horn sounded: "Mount and away."

He discovered that the mare needed no urging. With an effortless stride she kept well ahead. Across the recently plowed fields they went leaving deep scored hoof marks behind them, and Michael Karl found himself wondering, as he loosed his saber in its sheath and knotted its cord around his wrist, what the farmer would think when he came to view the ruin of his land.

They struck a road and turned down it in a flash. The Black Coats rode easily with taut reins holding back their eager horses for the last charge up the streets of Rein.

Before he knew it they were pounding down the pavement of New Rein and somewhere before them a shot or two told them that Grimvich was still busy.

The Inn of the Two Horses was barred and its

windows shuttered as were all the houses along the street. And then they were among the Legations. There were heads at the windows of the American Embassy, and from the balcony which hung above the British lion, a rash youngster leaned down to cheer them on with a shrill cry of "Good hunting!" after the flying heels.

Grimvich held the Bridge of the Flower Sellers, and from the windows of the neighboring houses his machine guns cracked and spit towards the darkened houses across the river where the enemy apparently had gone to earth. A soldier at the risk of being ridden down, dashed out to wave them to a stop, and Grimvich, as stolid as ever, came to stand at the stirrup of Michael Karl's plunging horse.

"His Majesty has been successful. The Fortress guns are silenced. Cobentz has withdrawn all but a few sharp-shooters from over there," he waved toward the houses across the bridge. "We follow you!" he had to shout to be heard.

Michael Karl nodded furiously and drew his saber. The soldier at the edge of the bridge jumped aside and they were on. Then the mare flew across the bridge with Urich's powerful roan at her flanks.

The Black Coats were firing without waiting for orders, swinging low from the saddle and coolly picking their targets. A man with a dirty bandage around his unkempt head fired wildly at Michael Karl as he swept by. Urich raised his rifle and shot. The man threw up his arms in a queer sort of way and slid down to lie very still with his head in the gutter.

A lone machine gun tried to stop them but the long rifles picked off its operators until it was abandoned, and two of the Black Coats, who had lost their mounts, put it to some good advantage against its former owners in a neighboring house. The first headlong speed of those who went on had slackened; they were forced to go more slowly because of the sharpshooters and snipers at the windows and in the dark doorways. But the bulk of Cobentz's force had gone, only a few disputed their passage.

But Michael Karl was wild with impatience. He must get to the Cathedral Square and hold it free for Grimvich's passage. From below came the crackle of rifle fire and the steady chatter of machine guns.

"Grimvich has entered the Bargo!" shouted Urich in his ear. Michael Karl set his jaw. Snipers or no snipers he was going to reach the Cathedral Square. He screamed to Urich, and the hunting horn sounded the "Charge!"

The horses' shoes struck sparks from the pavement and at the cost of two empty saddles they reached the avenue which ran into the Cathedral Square. Here and there a man could be seen firing desperately until he was picked off, but for the most part the Black Coats' small force was free from attack.

Some one spurred alongside of him. Michael Karl glanced around. A stranger in the shaggy pelt of a wolfman was shouting something and waving the banner, whose smooth silver Michael Karl had last seen draped above the throne, almost in his face.

"His Majesty holds the Fortress and most of Cobentz's ammunition, but he must have reinforcements. Cobentz has fortified the Cathedral. We must clear the Square!" Michael Karl at last made out the message.

"Does Cobentz have machine guns?" he almost burst his throat asking, but the wolfman shook his head, he didn't know.

The sound of firing was still coming from down the slope. Grimvich wasn't making a very quick advance, and their success or failure depended upon his being able to reach the King before Cobentz and the Reds rallied.

They were within a hundred feet of the Square now, but out of a side street burst a compact body of horse.

"The Household Guard," Urich pointed to them.

Michael Karl looked behind him. Every second man had drawn his saber while his mate held a rifle easily, spotting his target. They were in for it, but somehow he believed that the Household Guard was going to get the surprise of its life.

If they could meet them at the mouth of that side street before they could form to charge— Urich caught his thought and signaled the "Charge." There were a few feet of flying movement and then the shock of horse meeting horse and whirling steel clashing dizzily about them. Michael Karl thrust blindly and his saber came away red and sticky. A fat man in a brilliant uniform snarled into his face and then looked surprised, slipping limply downward in his saddle. The mare screamed shrilly and bit at the neck of a black, while the black's rider aimed a vicious blow

at Michael Karl's head. He tried to parry, but the
blade was in his very eyes and then it slipped away
and something stung his cheek.

Then they broke. As swiftly as they had come,
the guard turned and fled. He longed to order pur-
suit but the Square was yet to be taken. A horse
lay kicking on the pavement and he nodded with
dull approval when one of the Black Coats shot it
through the head.

A man lay face downward in a pool as scarlet
as his coat and Michael Karl, looking at him,
suddenly felt sick. One of the Black Coats was
sitting on the curb staring vacantly at a crimson
patch above his boot which spread stickily. Leaning against a house wall, dabbing at a wet patch on
his shoulder with a scrap of a white handkerchief,
was a youngster in a white and gold uniform. He
eyed Michael Karl sullenly.

"Your Highness is wounded!" Urich looked at
him anxiously. Michael Karl felt his cheek, and his
grimy hand came away red.

"It's nothing but a scratch. See to the injured,"
he motioned towards the sullen boy and the Black
Coat.

One of his men dismounted with a black case in
his hand and with help applied rough first-aid to
his comrade and their only prisoner. What to do
with the latter bothered Michael Karl. He dismounted and went over to him.

"Will you give your parole?" he asked. The boy
nodded and winced as the bandage was drawn
tighter across his shoulder.

Michael Karl unbuckled his belt and let it fall
with a clang. His recent bout had told him that it

was no use trying to fight in the tunic which drew so tightly over his shoulders every time he raised his arm. He slipped it off and stood in his shirt sleeves just as the rising sun touched the golden dome of the Cathedral.

Leaving the wounded Black Coat with the prisoner, they mounted and turned towards the Square.

Michael Karl felt like a person caught in a fantastic dream. The whole thing had lost its reality. As the mare moved forward he could hear the spitting of rifles from the lower town. He glanced back, twenty men still kept their saddles and five of them were slightly wounded. And with twenty men he had to take and hold the Square until Grimvich could join him, Grimvich who was moving with a deadly slowness.

Chapter XII

The Battle Of The Cathedral Steps

Cobentz had made good use of the time which had been allowed him, as Michael Karl saw when he clattered at the head of his little company to the end of the Avenue where it gave upon the Square. A barricade of boxes, splintered furniture, the loot of nearby homes, and some bales of scarlet and blue cloth from a wrecked shop, had been thrown up before the steps of the Cathedral itself, while from behind the barrier pointed sinister black rifle barrels.

Did they have machine guns? Michael Karl hesitating there knew that the success or failure of his job depended upon the answer to that question. If they did have them, he and his men would be mown down before they had crossed half the length of the Square. But then it was just as possible that Urlich Karl's quick and successful advance upon the Fortress had caught them sadly off guard and had left them but their rifles.

The Black Coats were beginning to waver and gather in indecisive little groups. Something must be done and done quickly or they would have to fall back and fail those who were depending upon them. And yet, if Cobentz had machine guns—

Michael Karl breathed deeply. He would have to try it. Dropping his revolver he leaned over in the saddle and snatched the Royal Standard out of the wolfman's lax grip. With a backward slash of his heels he scored the sides of the mare cruelly with his spurs.

She leaped like a hunted thing trying to get away from the agony of the steel. Straight into the Square and beyond she darted. Michael Karl shouted,

"The King! Morvania and the King!"

He thought that there was an answer from the barricade, a sullen growl, and from behind him came the faint shouts of his men. There were no machine guns. The mare gathered her feet beneath her and topped the barrier. Michael Karl caught a glimpse of a white twisted face and slashed down at it. Then the mare's shoes were drumming on the steps and he was using the pole of the Standard to ward off saber strokes. They dared not shoot for fear of wounding their own comrades crowding around him to pull him down.

The staff of the Standard snapped off short, five inches from his hand, as he was warding off a vicious blow from a ragged figure's clubbed rifle. He struggled to reach the top of the steps and the little band of bright coated officers where Cobentz must be.

Screaming shrilly the mare went down, a terrific blow of a rifle butt between her wild eyes. Michael Karl struggled free and like dogs they were on him to pull him down. He gained one step and then two; the carven niches of the saints were at his back. Turning to face the barricade he jammed his back and shoulders into one of the deep niches by the door and felt the bump when his head touched the stone feet of Saint Michael above him.

The little band of officers had disappeared and only the snarling wild men of the steps faced him. If they did not pick him off with a shot he was safe for a while.

Across the Square came the Black Coats, coolly firing as they came. The barricade had been cleared already, and its defenders were falling back sullenly while the horses of the dismounted Black Coats milled around the foot of the steps. Urich, his saber biting him a wide path, was coming up to him. It was close work, little shooting now, clubbed rifle against saber and revolver with the Black Coats winning out.

Michael Karl leaned against the cold stone, panting. For the moment they had forgotten him. He noted with a frown that the Royal Standard was a fringe of rags in his hand and that there was more then one dark stain on it. But he didn't have long to notice such small things.

A man in a peasant's blouse yelled hoarsely through his twisted mouth: "Get him before they get us!"

All his fellows within hearing, five or six of them, obeyed and they were at him. But a wicked saber met them with a will.

"Hold them!" screamed Urich from below. "Hold them!"

Michael Karl was trying hard, but it was an effort to raise his arm. The cut on his cheek ached cruelly and the sharp edges of the stone behind him pressed into his back. He was more aware of those discomforts than he was of the men who were trying to reach him.

The man with the twisted mouth shouted again and they drew back with a growl. Their leader raised his hand, Michael Karl guessed, and dropped, as the shot chipped one foot of the protecting saint above his head.

With a cry of victory his opponents turned to hurl themselves into the arms of Urich and the Black Coats. Urich, raving over what he supposed was Michael Karl's death, met them with naked steel, and when the Black Coats reached the next step there was silence and no opposition.

None had offered to surrender; the desperate men of the barricade had fought until a saber ripped them open or a bullet found them out. The Black Coats cleared the Cathedral steps, but ten of them were missing.

Michael Karl arose to his knees. It was very quiet now and the morning sun flashed the Cross on his breast to living fire. Down the hill the firing was dying out and at the edge of the Square the gray uniforms of the Legion began to appear.

He got up slowly, bracing himself with a hand against the stone. The Royal Standard lay crumpled at his feet and with some misgivings as to his balance he stooped over to pick it up. Urich and what was left of the Black Coats were watching him with dull wonder, as one who arose from the dead.

A scarlet trickle, growing larger every second,

made a miniature falls down the steps and in passing it splashed the boots of a Black Coat sitting limply and breathing very hard. Even as Michael Karl watched, the man sighed deeply and slid down to lie quietly on the pavement.

The mare, her smooth skin hacked and broken by the boots which had stamped over her, already lay there. Michael Karl looked down at her. She had served him well, and it seemed hard that all that grace and beauty should come to lie at the foot of the Cathedral steps soiled, and broken, and very still.

Urich came up to him walking slowly like an old man.

"They still hold the Cathedral, Your Highness. But they are just a handful, Cobentz and his officers."

So that was where the group of bright coated officers had disappeared when they saw that the game was against them.

Michael Karl rested his head against the Saint's toes wearily. They had won the steps and the Square but the Cathedral was yet to be taken.

"Call the roll," he said slowly.

Urich looked down at the Black Coats still on their feet. "There are ten of us, not counting Your Highness."

"We started with—"

"Forty, Your Highness."

Michael Karl looked across the Square. Beside the great fountain in the center lay a horse with his head in the water and with him a Black Coat. The defenders of the barrier had found their mark once at least. And now by the horse and his still rider, came in loose formation, the first of the Foreign Legion and with them, neat to his last shining button, Colonel Grimvich stalked very erect, swinging the swagger stick which was his badge of authority.

The Black Coats drew together at the top of the stairs with Michael Karl at their head, while the fruit of their hard won victory lay sprawled at their feet and across the barrier.

Grimvich paused as he caught sight of those horrible steps and then, looking upward, he touched his cane to his peaked cap in salute. Michael Karl answered with the hilt of the broken saber—the blade had snapped off when he had thrown himself down to escape the peasant's bullet—and then picked his way down to meet the Colonel.

"You found things a bit hot, Your Highness," observed the Colonel.

Michael Karl nodded. "Cobentz still holds the Cathedral, but your way is open. We'll smoke him out. Did you find hard going down below?"

Grimvich smiled for the first time since Michael Karl had met him.

"Rather. But we cleaned them out. We'll be on to the Fortress now. My beauties have enjoyed themselves this morning. Shall I leave you some reinforcements?"

"If you can spare me ten—" began Michael Karl hesitatingly as he looked up at the handful of Black Coats standing at the top of the steps.

"Nothing easier," said the Colonel heartily. "Cortlandt, ten men for His Highness. Haupthan is coming," Grimvich continued as the ten men were detached from the gray ranks and went to the barrier, "and the Duke is moving on the water pipes. Innesberg will be making terms within two days. Well, we're off. I'll inform His Majesty of what has been done here." Raising his cane in salute for the second time, the Colonel moved off, following his men up to the Fortress.

Michael Karl turned back to the Cathedral. It must be taken but, looking at its gray stone walls and massive doors of solid oak, he decided it was going to be a hard job.

He grasped the jagged broken blade of his saber and brought the massive guard down upon the door.

"In the name of the King, I call upon you to surrender!" he shouted.

They waited but the doors hung as blankly and silently closed as ever. Michael Karl knew that his demand for surrender was but a formality and expected no answer.

"For the last time I demand your surrender. The guns of the Fortress are trained upon the Cathedral." He hoped fervently that the guns could be. The Cathedral couldn't be taken with bare hands.

This time there was response, a dull roaring like the sound of the sea in a twisted shell. Something was evidently going on inside. Cobentz was a coward, but was he coward enough to throw open the Cathedral doors at what might be only an idle threat? But Michael Karl reckoned without the Archbishop.

To that little man the Cathedral was the world, that one stone of it be touched by shot was worse than sacrilege. At the very threat of such a thing he turned upon the defenders savagely.

There was a thud from within and the door swung back. Michael Karl blinked and tried to see through the gloom with his sun dazzled eyes. At the edge of the door was the wizened little figure in a red gown which he had last seen scudding away from the Council table swinging a silver cross which dangled from the chain in his hand.

The little figure looked blindly up, as confused by the light as Michael Karl was by the dark, his sunken mouth working pitifully and his thin arms spread out as if to protect the beauty of the church behind. Then seeming to see Michael Karl he stepped forward a pace, laying a yellow hand on the boy's arm.

"You will not hurt—hurt this?" he pleaded, motioning vaguely towards the dim beauty within. "The wicked ones are there, take them." He pointed to the high altar.

There was a sharp crack and the scarlet figure swayed limply against Michael Karl, but even as he fell he watched the boy's face hungrily for his answer.

"You will not hurt—" he whispered.

"I will not harm it," Michael Karl promised.

He sighed once very peacefully and then the Archbishop of Rein left the one thing he loved most of all, and a little figure in a red gown lay still against one of the beautiful columns of the Cathedral nave.

Michael Karl with Urich by his side and his men at his back entered. Once inside, they separated into two columns, one for each aisle, out of danger from a second shot. Now that his eyes were accustomed to the darkness Michael Karl could see the high altar and, on the steps below it, the little group of officers.

One of them shouted suddenly and the sound of his voice, echoed and reechoed, filling the whole Cathedral.

"Sanctuary! We claim sanctuary!"

Michael Karl thought of the red gowned figure by the door and went grimly on. When he noticed that one or two of the Black Coats were startled by the plea, he called in return:

"For those who break sanctuary, there is none. You murdered the Archbishop at his own door."

The Black Coats went on reassured. Those at the altar could hear their steady advance but could not see them. The pleader called again: "We throw down our arms. Will you make terms?"

Michael Karl answered remorselessly: "The time for making terms is past. If you surrender—perhaps."

"Would you shed blood here?" demanded the voice, now terror-stricken.

"You, yourself, have willed it so," answered Michael Karl.

And now from the altar they heard the sound of shuffling and a shout. Then the voice spoke again.

"We surrender and deliver Cobentz to you."

"March down the center aisle," commanded Michael Karl, still fearing treachery, "and bring him with you."

They came slowly, a sorry band in torn and stained uniforms. And among them, limp, his hands twisted behind his back with his own belt, Cobentz. His sly smile was gone, the yellow eyes stared unseeing straight before him, and there was foam on his purple lips.

The Black Coats stepped out and disarmed them, and shortly, bound and broken, they stood before Michael Karl. Cobentz was no longer even a man. He threw himself on the pavement and crawled to Michael Karl's boots making quavering animal sounds.

"Pity, pity!" he shrieked. Michael Karl turned away, sickened.

There was a rasp of spurs in the nave and Michael Karl looked up from the loathsome thing which had reached for the throne. One of the wolf-men was coming. He saluted Michael Karl.

"His Majesty states that the position is safe. He will be here in five minutes."

Michael Karl thanked him. Suddenly he felt very tired and ill. The mosaic pavement under his feet rocked up and down. When he tried to turn his head the cut on his cheek burned. He decided all at once that he didn't like war.

From the Square came the sound of cheering. Urlich Karl was coming. Michael Karl turned and walked unsteadily towards the door. Those steps should have been cleared.

But before he reached the door and its pitiful guardian, some one entered.

Michael Karl caught his breath. Surely this wasn't the American, this tall kingly figure in the scarlet coat and short, jewel buckled cape. He glanced down at his own ragged shirt where the diamond Cross bobbed up and down and at his blood splattered breeches. Then he looked up at the King's face with its charming smile and felt the brown hands which gripped his shoulders and heard the voice:

"Michael Karl, you aren't hurt?"

"I don't think so," answered Michael Karl, and all at once he felt very young, as if a great load of responsibility had been lifted from his thin shoulders.

"Well, if you aren't, boy, you ought to be," there was vast relief in the King's voice. "Your face is a sight."

"What have we here?" he demanded a moment later as, with his arm still about Michael Karl's shoulders, they came up to the prisoners. "Oh, Cobentz and Company. You made a very clean sweep, didn't you? We'll get rid of these for the moment."

He sent one of the wolfmen running for a prisoner's guard, and then he spoke to the Black Coats.

"I need not say it in words, Comrades, but you will find that this day's work will bring some fitting reward. You have saved a kingdom, and the king will remember it."

Michael Karl saw Urich jump forward and then he took no further interest in kings or kingdoms. Strong arms lifted him and there was a time when he seemed to be carried along halls and up stairs. Some one kept calling him, but for it all he fell asleep.

Something lay heavy across his breast and he put up his hands sleepily to push it away. The softness of velvet met his fingers. He turned and opened his eyes. There was a fireplace big enough for the whole of a small log, a high-backed chair with a crest in faded gilt on its back. Michael Karl watched them drowsily and then he looked up.

Above the heavy mantel hung a picture. A slim boy with laughing eyes and rumpled black hair held the reins of a spirited black horse, while, at his mud splattered, booted feet, two hounds lolled, their tongues drooling from the open jaws as if they had but finished the hunt. Their master's white breeches were mud-stained, and his hunting coat was ripped on the shoulder, but, from his fingers dangled the coveted "brush."

Michael Karl studied the boy. His face was familiar. Was he one of the officers he had met on the avenue or at the Cathedral? He didn't think so. A lad like that wouldn't be mixed up with Cobentz and his rotten gang. It was probably some one he had seen at Urlich Karl's camp in the mountains.

By the way, where was he now? He rolled over on his back and studied the green velvet canopy over his head. The last thing he remembered with any certainty was standing in the Cathedral, with the king's arm about him, watching the pillars whirl around in a crazy sort of way.

He looked down the green velvet cover between the carved bedposts. Another chair faced him, but this time it was completely filled by a sleeping wolfman. He had tossed back the tight, hairy hood-mask and had pillowed his head on his arm. Michael Karl watched him but it was very plain that he wasn't going to sit up and be an interesting companion for some time.

Michael Karl turned his head stiffly. The whole side of his face ached, and he discovered with investigating fingers that it was tightly bandaged.

This side of the room was occupied by two more high-backed chairs, a long table carved with a hunting scene all the way around its edge, and a heavy chest. Above the table, balancing the boy of the hunt on the other side of the room, was another deep frame and heavy canvas. Again it was a boy staring down at Michael Karl, but there was no good humor in his arrogant eyes or charming smile curving his thin lips.

"A very unpleasant person," commented Michael Karl aloud as he studied the portrait.

"And that he was, boy. I saw quite a lot of him." The king was standing at the foot of the bed with the wolfman still sleeping behind him.

Michael Karl looked up at his cousin without surprise. He was used to these sudden appearances.

"Who was he?"

"Our grandfather, the late king. I have yet to find a single person who liked him. And that one," he nodded towards the boy of the hunt, "is Prince Eric, your father. You're amazingly like him. That might be a picture of you. How do you feel after helping to conquer a city?"

"Fine and—and dandy. See here, I want to get up."

"All in good time. You gave us the fright of our lives, young man, when you decided to pass out of the picture in the Cathedral. Urich got quite angry with me for not sending reinforcements sooner. You've made a large number of loyal supporters for yourself, boy. I shall have to have you take the oath of allegiance as soon as possible because, if you decided to rebel, I would find myself out in the cold world before I knew what happened. How does it feel to be a hero?"

"Oh, rot! What did you do with Cobentz and the rest?"

Urlich Karl's eyes lost their dancing lights, and his jaw seemed to sharpen.

"Cobentz will be tried for treason and the murder of the Archbishop. Either way we've got him. The rest we'll probably exile."

"And Innesberg?"

"Surrendered this morning. The mere threat of cutting off the water supply brought them to terms. They hadn't any good leaders after Kamp was killed when we took the Fortress. Of course, the trouble in the south isn't over yet, but we can safely leave it to Johann. He's suddenly produced an iron hand for ruling which is earning him a lot of respect and wholesome fear.

"I'm through with a native Household Guard though for the late one turned traitor to a man. The Wolf Pack shall be the bodyguard, and the Foreign Legion will hold the Fortress. I can depend on them.

"By the way, the part of your own regiment which remained loyal to the Council is suing for forgiveness and peace. I told them that I'd leave them to you."

"How about Laupt and Kafner?"

A shadow of a frown wrinkled the King's smooth forehead.

"We can't find them. I know that they haven't left the country. It's their being at large that worries me. Laupt was the brains of this whole affair, and I shan't breathe easily until I get him under lock and key in the Lion Tower."

"You'll get him," answered Michael Karl

promptly. After the taking of Rein he firmly believed that this tall young man, perched without
dignity on the foot of his bed, could do anything he
wanted to.

"Now tell me," he commanded, "about how you
took the Fortress."

Chapter XIII

Who Holds Rein Holds Morvania

"No," he corrected himself, "tell me how you became a quick change artist, Werewolf to American to King. I don't like stories which begin in the middle and—"

"Run both ways?" supplied his cousin. "Well, all this mess is due to the mismanagement of the late but not lamented King, our ungracious grandparent. He was a domestic tyrant of no mean order, modeled himself on the father of Frederick the Great. I won't go so far as to say that he threw plates at the heads of Princes of the Blood or tore their clothes off their backs, but he did his best to make this Fortress a merry little hell for any one who was unfortunate enough to be a relation of his.

"He bullied his wife to death and then started in on his sons. One morning he tramped into breakfast and jumped on Prince Eric, your father. Eric, of course, was a younger son, and he had no desire for the throne anyway, so he waited until the old man paused for breath and then gave him as good as he got, ending up by declaring that Prince or no

Prince he was going to America and he'd like to see his father try to stop him.

"The King sat there in a sort of stunned silence like a cat who had been badly bitten by a mouse it was playing with. Prince Eric calmly finished his breakfast and stated he was going to pack. His father didn't try to stop him then, maybe he had a sneaking liking for the only member of his family who had ever told him what was what, or maybe he was just temporarily out of commission from shock.

"Eric bid every one good-by including his brother Stefan, the Crown Prince. The last thing he said to Stefan was to advise him to get out while the going was good. However, Stefan had some ties, not the least of which was yours truly who was raising an awful row in the Royal nursery about then.

"Prince Eric just got across the border when the officer sent to arrest him arrived at the frontier post. I think Karl had planned a taste of the Lion Tower for Eric when he made that last grab after his fast-moving son.

"Old Karl sort of simmered after that. He didn't smash things but he looked as if he were going to at any minute, and everybody within hearing got in the habit of tiptoeing around and trying to look like statues when the King favored them with his attention. It was dreadfully wearing on the nerves, like waiting for a delayed bomb to go off.

"They didn't have to wait long. Eric sailed for America, reached New York and disappeared.

"The King raged—one of his family had defied him and had gotten away with it. He immediately started a search for him. I hate to think what detective bills the state had to pay.

"After almost two years he was finally located, going under an assumed name of course. And when the King ordered him home at once, he said firmly that he was sorry but he intended staying right there because he was to be married the next month, and he didn't think his bride would like Morvania. Anyway he was more interested in working in his father-in-law's steel mills than he was in playing the role of Prince, and he wanted to study to be an engineer.

"That finished the King. There was one grand explosion and people went around picking up pieces of their self-esteem for months afterwards. My father used a little of Eric's medicine and politely but firmly withdrew to his castle in the mountains. He said that he was through having his child scared into fits by his father stamping and yelling up and down the halls.

"The King never mentioned Eric again and he didn't rage so much. After my father was killed in a landslide, he had me put in school and I never saw him again but for a few minutes at a time every five years or so.

"About a year and a half after the message from Eric, the King commanded that all the Prince's pictures be draped in black and had a mass sung in the Cathedral. He didn't give out any information but every one knew that the Prince was dead.

"Things were in an awful mess. All the worthwhile element of the nobility were on their estates, exiled for speaking favorably of the missing Prince.

"Laupt, Kafner, Oberdamnn, and their ilk were making hay and making it to some purpose. We were neutral during the war and some mighty queer people and things leaked over the border in the last few months before the armistice. Kamp suddenly appeared from the North. He had had a big hand in the Russian mixup.

"The King was so busy making things unpleasant for the few people who were still loyal to him that he didn't have time to check up on the various tricks of Laupt and Company. Kamp he treated as a joke, and that made Kamp see red. He was used to having aristocrats tremble in their shoes at the mere mention of his name, so the King's indifference stung him into some really brilliant underground work.

"In every country there's always a few who begin to look excited when some one suggests taking things from the rich and giving them to the poor. But up to 1930 we hadn't had much trouble. Innesberg had revolted once or twice, of course, but it was the usual thing, and nobody became alarmed about it, just as no one becomes excited about a revolution in a South American republic; it was an old story. However, there were the embers, and Kamp set about fanning them into a good roaring fire.

"There was a strike in the factories, and some of the old time owners used the iron hand a little too heavily. They had to call out the guard, and the King made matters worse by arriving on the scene and taking charge over the protests of his officers. Then Kamp finished his rebellion by having the . King shot. The Morvanians will stand for a lot, but they have some old-fashioned notions and one of them is a sturdy loyalty to the throne. They could stand revolution but not king murder.

"Kamp saw that he had overplayed his hand. He disappeared and Laupt and Company came into the feast licking their chops.

"I was in the mountains the week before the King left for Innesberg. You know the law: the Heir must claim the throne within a month or the Council steps in for a year. It was made during the Middle Ages when each ruling Duke had six or seven sons and there were a lot of quiet murders. Kafner saw his chance and took it. Unfortunately for him there were still some men loyal to the throne among his intimates. One of them warned me and I proceeded to disappear.

"Johann came to Rein and started working. He couldn't understand what they were going to do at the end of the year, when they didn't have any heir to produce. You see, none of us knew that Eric had a son. Johann suspected that I was alive and managed to get in touch with me. He was dreadfully afraid that they were going to put up Cobentz.

"Then Kafner sprang the bomb of your existence upon the Council, and Johann was worried. You weren't hated like Cobentz, you were nearer the throne, and your father had been very popular with the people. Unless something happened I was in a pretty tough place. Every one who would have supported me thought I was dead and the minute I dared appear again I was a target for one of Laupt's assassins.

"That was when I became the American reporter. I had to be in Rein some of the time, and that was the ideal role. Everybody thought I was writing a book and that gave me license to poke around in all sorts of queer places—"

"But weren't you ever recognized?" demanded Michael Karl.

Urlich Karl laughed. "It was really very simple; the people expect a king to wear a bright uniform and ride a horse, never appearing in public without a bodyguard, they can't imagine a king in a business suit poking around in cathedrals and ruined castles for story material. It was the old case of hiding something by putting it in plain sight.

"Then, too, the way I had been brought up helped a lot. I'd never been around the court much, for I was on our mountain estate until my father died, and then I went straight to military school in Cambsilt, a little town at the head of the Laub. Hardly any one knew what I looked like. And of course I was dead and why look for a dead man."

"But why an American? You were never in America were you?"

The King shook his head. "No, but my tutor was an American, and I always admired him. And I always read American books and papers. I had a soldier of fortune who drifted into my Wolf Pack drill me in up-to-date slang, and there aren't very many other Americans in Morvania to compare me with.

"The Werewolf idea I got from old mountain legends. It helped me among the peasants and discouraged spies. Even Johann didn't know that I was playing that part as well; he thought that the

Werewolf was one of my former aides-de-camp."

Urlich Karl paused to explain.

"The Werewolf legend is well known in the mountains. A werewolf is an evil creature something like a vampire who has the power of becoming a wolf from sunset to sunrise during which time he is supposed to seek men to devour.

"There are many ways of becoming a werewolf. If you drink from a stream where wolves have lapped, if you eat the brains of a wolf, if you pick and wear a certain sort of flower, if you wear the belt of a werewolf, and if you summon the demon wolf himself to give you the power. I summoned the demon wolf."

"What!"

Urlich Karl nodded seriously. "Our mountain peasants are a shrewd lot. You must be the real thing, they have no time for shams. Yes, I summoned the demon wolf following the instructions of a wise woman. It's a rather complicated ceremony, but I had quite a few hidden witnesses who went home and reported that I was the genuine article.

"Look." From beneath his tunic he drew a smooth belt of gray wolf hide fastened with a gold clasp.

"Don't put it around you," he warned Michael Karl laughingly, "if you don't want to become a werewolf."

"But what do you mean 'demon wolf'?" questioned Michael Karl excitedly twisting the belt in his hands.

His cousin grew serious. "I don't know. I saw nothing or heard nothing. But then I was just going through the ceremony to impress my hidden listeners. I can not tell you whether the demon wolf really made his appearance or not. I would never do it again. Most of those old mountain legends have a grain of truth behind them. Perhaps there is a demon wolf. But I did not see him. Nor am I a true Werewolf. See."

He held out his hands. "Were I a true werewolf, my nails would be long and scarlet, glittering in the light. And my eyebrows would slant up to meet in a point above my nose. But you see I failed to make the proper connections, and I am still human. But the mountaineers listen for my howling each night.

"The wolf mask gave me the wolf head that a werewolf must have."

"But the real wolves?" broke in Michael Karl.

"Yes, those who followed the horses were the finishing touch, weren't they? There were ten of them in all. An old mountain shepherd, by the way he was supposed to be a real werewolf, caught and tamed them when they were cubs. We never quite trusted them though."

"And the Wolf Pack?"

"They were mountaineers loyal to the throne, deserters from the army who wanted to follow me, and one or two soldiers of fortune who later went to form the beginning of the Foreign Legion. And never has a Prince been served so well as the Wolf Pack served me."

"So that is how the Werewolf started," said Michael Karl looking down at the belt in his hands. "Here goes," he added suddenly and twisted the belt about him. "Now watch me, Werewolf!'' he challenged his cousin.

"And what did you think about my coming?" he questioned a moment later.

"Well, when we found out about you we didn't know what to do. Johann wanted to let them bring you to Rein as they had planned and then take care of you, but I thought it would be better to get you in the mountains. We didn't know much about you or what you would do, but we thought that it would be safer to act on the idea that you were an enemy.

"The affair of the halfway station was too simple. Kafner of course wasn't prepared, and it was the easiest thing in the world to stop the train. Only, when my men searched it, they couldn't find you, and when they did snatch you up they believed that you were one of the royal aides-de-camp. We thought we'd throw a scare into you and let you go in a couple of days to give Laupt something to think about.

"Then when we found we had the right man after all—"

"You tried to frighten him to death," ended Michael Karl.

His cousin smiled ruefully. "I did make it rather strong, didn't I? I had some hopes you would take the hint and go back to America. We were going to give your choice the next day between imprisonment and a ticket back to America. And then you complicated things by escaping.

"The Pack were afraid that you'd get far enough down the valley to arouse the frontier posts. Those near shots weren't misses, my men can shoot better than that even at night, they were warnings.

When you banged in on me I didn't know what to do, but you made it so plain that you were sick of Morvania that I decided to see you through the mess."

"Why didn't you tell me who you were and let me out of the whole thing right then?"

"Well," Urlich Karl hesitated and then smiled shyly, "I rather liked what I saw of you and I didn't want to lose you right away. Royal princes are very lonely people, Michael Karl. I never in my life had a friend near my own age. Even when I went to school I was not allowed to mix with the rest of the boys because they weren't my equals in rank. And then when you came—"

"You decided to put up with me," finished Michael Karl triumphantly. "I should think you were sick of your bargain by now," he added laughingly.

"I have never once regretted your coming," answered the King slowly, and Michael Karl felt very happy all of a sudden.

"You know the rest of the story until we parted at the camp. I'll say frankly that I never expected that you would have any trouble taking the Cathedral Square—"

"Or you would never have allowed me to do it," said Michael Karl shrewdly.

"Right you are," admitted Urlich Karl. "Do you think I want to lose you, of all people?"

"We had no trouble getting into the city. The people were with us, they had no taste for Cobentz. It wasn't until we took the Fortress that their forces concentrated upon holding the Cathedral Square. There was some little resistance at the head of the Pala Horn, but my wolves were old hands at the game, and we were through quickly.

"Jan was scared stiff when we came banging in upon him. He was with Breck and Kanda at the door, and they were prepared to sell their lives dearly. I shall never forget the dear man's face when I lifted my wolf mask."

"So you used the secret passage?"

"Yes. It was beautifully simple. The hall, the throne room, and the gun room were ours before they noticed and some officers who were secretly loyal helped us corner the ammunition supply. We were holding the Fortress, precariously, but still holding it, within ten minutes. Cobentz was down in the city somewhere and my men couldn't find Laupt, Kafner or the General. I couldn't detach too many to search and there were lots of bolt-holes that we stopped too late.

"Grimvich got up to us, and then I breathed easier. It's no fun trying to hold a place of this size with a hundred men. He told me about the difficulties in the Square, and I was preparing to send you reinforcements when the news came that the Cathedral was taken.

"Thanks to you all I had to do was put Cobentz and the rest under lock and key. And then you ended the whole thing by passing out peacefully. You gave me a bad five minutes then, boy."

"Then the fighting is over?" asked Michael Karl.

"If you could step out on your balcony this minute you would see flags and other signs of rejoicing all over the place. Yes, our war has been won. Feeling rather disappointed, aren't you? But you had your storming of the Cathedral, and you mustn't be greedy."

"What of the Lion Tower?"

Urlich Karl's answer was grim. "We freed certain prisoners who will take pleasure in seeing the end of Cobentz. It seems that he did not have nerve enough to kill those he hated if they were highly placed, he just kept them in his dungeons. There is much of a medieval tyrant about Cobentz."

The King leaned back against the bed post and traced a raised design on the velvet cover with his finger.

"Have you any idea what you are going to do now?" he asked without looking up.

Michael Karl shook his head. He had a queer disappointed feeling as if he had made some wonderful plans, but when he came to act upon them found that they weren't so wonderful after all. Drearily he supposed it was what was called "reaction."

"You'll stay on until after the coronation won't you?" asked his cousin.

"Do you think," replied Michael Karl, "that I would miss seeing you on the throne after I had worked as hard as I have to put you there?"

The King gave a little sigh, perhaps of relief, and when he looked up his eyes were full of the old time dancing lights.

"Then, that is off my mind," he said a little hastily. "If we can locate Laupt—"

"Why, Your Majesty?"

Urlich Karl swung around and Michael Karl sat bolt upright. The guard in the wolf skin had lifted his head from his arm and was eyeing them coolly.

Michael Karl had seen those black, deeply sunken eyes and thin cruel lips before.

"Laupt!" said the King very softly.

"Just so," said the Major with a twisted smile. "I wouldn't look at that bell cord if I were you, Your Majesty. If you wish to reach for it. do, and I shall be forced to shoot. Not at you, of course, but at His Highness."

The dull colored revolver in his hand swung up a trifle until it pointed straight at Michael Karl's bandaged head.

"I am a crack shot, Your Majesty."

"What do you want?" There was ice below the smoothness of the King's voice.

"Just your signature on this, Your Majesty." He held out a slip of paper and, as Urlich Karl hesitated, he added, "By all means read it, you will not find it unreasonable."

Urlich Karl read it swiftly and passed it to his cousin. It was a pass for three beyond the lines and over the border.

"And if I refuse?"

Laupt smiled again, and Michael Karl leaned back on his pillows. Laupt's smile was anything but a pleasant sight.

"I don't think you will. Unless you sign that I haven't a chance, and I know it. My life is forfeit to the Crown. Under those conditions," he spoke very slowly, straight at Urlich Karl, "under those conditions what is there to prevent my firing one shot? Just one shot, Your Majesty, and I promise that you will not be touched."

"I agree," answered Urlich Karl clearly.

"I thought you would," purred Laupt.

"But what is there to prevent my countermanding this the moment you have left us?"

"Nothing, Your Majesty. But there is nothing either to prevent my leaving certain instructions. I still have followers in the Bargo for all your cleaning up. If you value your cousin's life, you will give me three hours' start, Your Majesty."

Urlich Karl went over to the table and opened the drawer. There was a quill pen and a bottle of half-dried ink.

Then Michael Karl found his voice. "Don't do it," he commanded. "It's a bluff."

"So." Laupt pulled the trigger. There was a faint pop and something scorched Michael Karl's cheek and bored a round hole in the pillow.

"The next time," said Laupt, "I shall fire a little to the right."

Michael Karl touched his cheek. A few drops of blood sprinkled his pajama collar.

"You don't dare," he said to Laupt.

The man paid no attention to him. "Sign," he commanded roughly.

Urlich Karl dipped his pen in the ink. For a fraction of a second Laupt's eye wavered. Then Michael Karl saw. Behind Laupt the door was opening inch by inch. The King was taking a long time over his signature, and Michael Karl knew that he knew.

From the half-open door, hands shot out and caught Laupt by the throat. At Urlich Karl's warning cry Michael Karl flung himself forward face down while a bullet made a black hole in the hollow of the pillow where his head had rested. The shaggy fur pelt kept the attacker from getting a good hold on Laupt's throat and the man was attempting to fire again, this time at Urlich Karl. He was desperate. As he had told Urlich Karl, he knew that there was no mercy for him, and another death more or less meant nothing to him.

Urlich Karl dropped lightly to the floor and then made a sudden tackle. The heavy chair went over with a crash and Laupt's assailants went down with him. There was a confused jumble on the floor and then a shot. One of the struggling figures rolled back limply.

The King arose panting and after him one of the Foreign Legion stumbled to his feet. Laupt lay grinning up at them, a shred of gray cloth between his set teeth. He had fought like an animal. Urlich Karl picked up the gun and tossed it on the table. It fell with a faint clang.

"Is he—?" questioned Michael Karl.

His cousin nodded. "Yes, he's dead and it's better all around. Get him out of here, Langley."

The soldier saluted and then dragged and pushed the body into the hall. An officer rapped at the half-open door, and at the King's command he entered.

"The airplane has disappeared, Your Majesty," he reported. "We have found a boy who saw two men getting into it, and we have reason to believe that they were Count Kafner and General Oberdamnn."

"Thank you," the King answered curtly. "You will, of course, advise the frontier posts. But," he added, more to himself than to the officer, "I don't think we'll hear of either of them again."

When the officer had tramped out he turned to

Michael Karl. "So they double-crossed him. He staked everything on his chance, and that pass was made out for the three of them. And while he was here they deserted them. Laupt had courage. Had he had as much loyalty to the throne as he had to his worthless friends, he would have supported me as staunchly as Johann.

"Kamp is dead, and so is Laupt. Oberdamnn and Kafner are beyond our justice, and I think that they will not be eager to return. The revolution is finished. The yellow roses will find the sun very nourishing."

"It was fun," said Michael Karl a bit wistfully, "while it lasted."

The cut on his cheek throbbed. "I say, won't I look the proper ruffian at your coronation if both these things," he motioned toward either cheek, "leave scars?"

"We'll have to see about that." Urlich Karl stepped lightly over and pulled at the bell cord.

As in the old days Jan answered it, but a transformed Jan. A white wig framed his round smooth face and a maroon, gold-laced coat pinched in his plump shoulders. He beamed on them like an amiable frog.

"Ask Dr. Wooner to step here," Urlich Karl ordered. With the familiar bob of his head Jan disappeared.

"It seems like home to see Jan," said Michael Karl.

"Then the house on the Pala Horn was home to you?"

"Of course," answered Michael Karl.

Urlich Karl hesitated, but before he could

speak, Jan sidled in and announced:

"Dr. Wooner."

The King stepped forward to meet the man in the gray uniform of the Foreign Legion.

"My cousin has had another accident," he explained laughingly, "and he is worried for fear it will spoil his beauty. Reassure him, Doctor."

Michael Karl promptly ran out his tongue as far as it would go at His Majesty, the King of Morvania.

Chapter XIV

The Last Of Cobentz And Co.

Michael Karl pulled back his shoulders so that the wrinkles across the breast of his black tunic smoothed out nicely, and reached out for the silk sash which took the place of a sword belt.

"Very nice, v-e-r-y nice," he drawled. "Don't you think so, Urich?"

The tall youngster whose black tunic matched Michael Karl's own agreed vehemently.

"And now I'll trouble you for that Cross if you please. I can't seem to get rid of the thing."

Urich handed him the Cross of Sebastian. Michael Karl glanced around the luxurious room and then at his own sable and gold magnificence.

"Not much like the last time I wore it," he observed and leaned forward a little to look closely into the mirror. On one cheek was the faint pink mark which showed the path of Laupt's bullet and which Dr. Wooner had assured him would disappear altogether in a couple of weeks. But nothing would ever erase the white scar which the skirmish on the Avenue had given him.

The scar wasn't the only change on his face. It

was a little thinner and a great deal older. He was becoming quite grown up.

"Admiring your beauty?" Urich jumped to attention as the King, with Johann lounging at his heel as sleepy as ever, entered.

Michael Karl colored. "You would say that," he began.

"But you really do look charming, my boy." The King raised an imaginary eyeglass and surveyed him through it. "That uniform is very becoming. You should always wear black."

Michael Karl put his forefingers in the corners of his eyes and pulled them down at the same time making his tongue protrude, the whole making a perfectly disgusting face. The King eyed him a moment and then—

"I can do much better than that," he said and proceeded to do it.

Duke Johann spoke languidly. "Of course, I have no intention of interrupting Your Majesty, but we have business at ten and"—he glanced at his watch, not the one he had lent to Michael Karl, for that had been hopelessly smashed during the fight on the steps, but another which that young gentleman had sent him—"it is almost the hour now."

"I have heard my master's voice," laughed the King and running his arm through Michael Karl's he led the way out of the room.

"What's all the excitement about?" asked Michael Karl. His cousin grew serious.

"We are going to see the last of Cobentz and Co."

They passed down wide halls and corridors adding to their train of brilliant attendants every minute. Sentries presented arms with a crash and jingle of metal which sounded and resounded through the halls. Powdered footmen bent almost double. It was all very exciting.

"Quite like a circus parade, isn't it?" whispered the King. "All we need is an elephant or two. Thank goodness you're here, I don't know what I'd do without you for a safety valve. And here we are."

They paused before a great door which two footmen jumped to open. An elderly gentleman in a black satin court suit with a gold rod of office in his hand stepped forward.

"His Majesty, Urlich Karl Franz Erich Roaul, by the Grace of God, King of Morvania, Overlord of the Seven Provinces, and Grand Duke of Rein!"

There was a distant murmur from the other side of the door where the gentleman in black was standing. Michael Karl could see his back and his arms move as he raised his staff of office the second time.

"His Highness, Michael Karl Johann Stefan Rene Erich Marie, Prince of Rein!"

The King stepped forward. His face had smoothed into a mask, and he had become another and rather terrifying person. The man in black satin moved aside and they were standing inside the door at the head of a flight of stairs, Michael Karl the regulation two paces behind the King.

They were in a great paneled hall overhung by two crowded galleries. Down either side, with a red carpeted aisle between, were arranged two lines of high-backed carven chairs and at the end of the hall was a dais upon which stood a solitary throne-like chair. A little to one side was a second

chair a step lower and before the whole a long
table with a bench at either end.

"The Judgment Hall of Rein," Urich whispered.

The men who had occupied the side chairs were
standing as were the throngs in the packed
galleries. Sweeping down the steps the King
walked down the center aisle and took his seat on
the throne. Michael Karl, he motioned toward the
chair a step lower.

On the table below the King's dais lay a
sheathed sword, a ponderous two-handed thing
from the days of the Crusades. Beside it lay a
simple peeled willow wand which Johann now
reached for. The King nodded his head, and there
was a rustle as all in the hall seated themselves.

Johann stepped out into the center aisle.

"Let the prisoner enter," he called.

At a side door there was the clink of arms and
two men, whose green tunics were embroidered
with black wolf heads, stepped in, Cobentz between them. Like a sleep-walker he stared straight
before him, and one of the guards had to guide
him into position before Johann.

The Duke began to speak.

"In the early days when the ruling Duke
traveled through all Morvania, giving justice to all
who asked it of him, the Courts of Rein were in the
open fields and men brought peeled willow wands
as a sign of pleading at those courts. Do you, Henri
Charles, wish to plead before the Courts of Rein?"

Like one moving in a dream the Marquisa took
the willow wand from Johann and turned to face
the assembly.

"My lords and gentlemen," he said in a high thin

voice, "I, by my birthright as a Lord of the Court, demand to be tried by my fellow Lords before the High Court of Rein."

Then he faced around once more and tossed the stick on the table so that it fell across the sword.

"The charge," commanded the Duke.

A tall man in a white curled wig and a plain black gown arose from one of the table benches and produced a rolled parchment.

"It is stated," he began to read aloud in a dry crackling voice, "that during the year of the regency of the High Council of Rein, Henri Charles, born Marquisa and Lord of Cobentz, did wrongly and wantonly conspire against the person of the Crown Prince and against the rule of the regents by inciting rebellion, and while under arms during such a rebellion, this same Henri Charles did wickedly and malicously put to death His Grace, the Archbishop of Rein."

The thin man rolled up his parchment with a snap and retired to his seat.

"What does the prisoner plead?" asked the Duke.

Another bewigged and gowned figure arose from the opposite side of the table and replied in a hoarse voice: "He pleads not guilty, Your Grace."

"Prisoner before the High Court of Rein, are you prepared to stand trial?"

Cobentz muttered inaudibly and took his seat in a chair at one side. The Duke turned to the throne.

"The prisoner is ready for trial, Your Majesty."

"Then call the witnesses," commanded Urlich Karl.

Urich leaned across the back of Michael Karl's

chair. "Be ready, Your Highness. The witnesses are called according to rank and you are first. When your name is read, step down into the center aisle and face the hall."

Michael Karl had just time enough to hiss back "Thank you," when Johann called, "His Highness, Michael Karl, Prince of Rein."

Michael Karl obeyed Urich's instructions and stepped down into the center aisle.

"Do you swear upon the honor of your house that what you are about to say is the truth?" asked the Duke sternly.

Michael Karl's "I do!" quavered a little with excitement.

"Did Your Highness receive certain orders from His Majesty on the night that His Majesty took the city of Rein?"

"I did."

"Repeat those orders to the Court if you please, Your Highness."

"I was to wait for the green rocket from the bridge and then enter with my men and go straight to the Cathedral Square, holding it open that His Majesty might receive reinforcements in the Fortress."

"What happened when Your Highness reached the Cathedral Square?"

"A body of the Household Horse attempted to stop us, but we won through to find that the rebels had fortified the Cathedral and barricaded the approach to it."

"With what result did Your Highness attack the barricade?"

"We took it with a large loss."

"Was the Marquisa Cobentz among Your Highness's prisoners at the end of the engagement?"

"There were no prisoners," answered Michael Karl slowly.

At his answer there was a murmur through the hall.

"Had Your Highness given any orders that there were to be no prisoners?"

Michael Karl shook his head. "No. The rebels refused to surrender and fought to the end. There was no cry for quarter from either side."

"After Your Highness had swept the barricade what occurred?"

"Colonel Grimvich and the Foreign Legion reached the Square. The Colonel informed me that His Majesty seemed to be holding out successfully and that he would report the progress made in the Square when he reached His Majesty. He offered me reinforcements which I accepted. I had but ten men left."

"How many men did Your Highness have when you left His Majesty's mountain camp?"

"Forty."

Again Michael Karl heard the murmur of the listeners.

"When Your Highness received reinforcements from Colonel Grimvich what did you do?"

"My men informed me that the Marquisa Cobentz and his officers had withdrawn into the Cathedral. I rapped on the door and called upon them to surrender. There was no answer. Then I threatened them with the Fortress guns."

"With what result, Your Highness?"

"His Grace, the Archbishop, fearing for the

safety of the Cathedral, opened to us. He informed us that the rebels were by the High Altar; a moment later he was shot."

"Did Your Highness then make preparations to take the Marquisa and his officers?"

"I did. My party separated and a group went up each aisle out of sight of the rebels. They called to us that they had taken sanctuary. I replied that the murder of His Grace denied them sancturary. One of them called again that they had disarmed the Marquisa and were coming down to surrender."

"Did they do so?"

"They did."

"What was the attitude of the Marquisa Cobentz when he was brought before you?"

Michael Karl flushed. "He seemed unlike himself."

"In what manner was he unlike himself, Your Highness?"

"He seemed very much afraid."

"What orders did Your Highness give concerning the Marquisa?"

"That he should be guarded. His Majesty then arrived and took charge."

"His Majesty thanks Your Highness for your cooperation with the Crown in answering these inquiries. Has the Defense any questions to ask?"

The man in the black gown, who had entered Cobentz's plea of not guilty, arose and turned to the throne.

"If it please Your Majesty," he began, "the Defense has certain questions to put to His Highness. Have we Your Majesty's gracious permission to proceed?"

"The Defense may proceed," answered Urlich Karl.

Duke Johann stepped back and seated himself at the table while the black gown took his place.

"Your Highness has stated that you acted upon the direct orders of His Majesty in taking the Cathedral Square?"

"That is true."

"Was Your Highness wounded in the engagement which took place directly before you reached the Square?"

"I received a slight scratch on one cheek. Nothing serious."

"Your Highness bears a scar from that wound?"

"I do."

For the life of him Michael Karl couldn't understand what the smooth voiced lawyer was attempting to prove. However, it wouldn't be a bad plan to be wary, very wary.

"During the engagement upon the steps of the Cathedral, did Your Highness ever lose your footing?"

"I ducked once to escape a bullet."

"Was that bullet fired by one of the officers commanding the rebels?"

Michael Karl shook his head. "The party of officers had disappeared before that."

"Aha—" The lawyer sucked in his breath with a purring sound.

"Was Your Highness ever close enough to distinguish any individual among those officers?"

Michael Karl thought furiously. Had he seen any one of the men well enough to remember him? No, all he could see when he closed his eyes was the five or six bright tunics at the head of the stairs, but he couldn't recall a single face.

"Does Your Highness remember any single one of those officers well enough to describe him?"

"No," said Michael Karl at last. "I remember seeing them, but I don't remember any of their faces."

Again the lawyer sighed his pleased little "ha."

"Then it might be possible that the Marquisa Cobentz was not one of those officers?"

"But he was!" protested Michael Karl.

"Will Your Highness swear to that?" the lawyer caught him up.

"I can't," said Michael Karl miserably. He saw what the fellow was doing. "But one of my men probably can."

"You can not answer for your men, Your Highness."

"If the Marquisa wasn't among the officers on the steps, how did he get into the Cathedral?" counter-questioned Michael Karl.

"The Crown will have the right to put such questions later, Your Highness," the lawyer rebuked him.

"When Your Highness stepped in, and the Archbishop was shot, did Your Highness see the Marquisa fire that shot?"

Again Michael Karl was forced to answer "No."

"After the Marquisa and his companions were taken, did Your Highness become ill from exhaustion?"

"Yes."

"Isn't it true that owing to Your Highness' condition it is hard for Your Highness to remember the events of that day clearly?"

"No, it is not!" snapped Michael Karl with some heat.

"That is all, Your Majesty," said the lawyer and retired.

Urlich Karl leaned forward. "On behalf of the Crown we thank Your Highness for your prompt and ready assistance. Your Highness is excused."

Michael Karl bowed, stepped back and seated himself.

"I made a hash of it, didn't I?" he whispered to Urich.

"He got two admissions very damaging to our case out of Your Highness," he admitted gravely. "But I don't see how Your Highness could have answered any differently."

"But the King or Johann could tell them something!"

"They can't because of their positions. Johann is the hereditary prosecutor of the court and the King is the judge. Neither of them can go on the witness stand."

"Baron Urich von Brunn," summoned Johann.

Urich stepped down to take his place in the center aisle.

"You acted as His Highness's aide-de-camp upon the taking of Rein?"

"I did."

"You were with His Highness when he fought his way up the Cathedral steps?"

"No."

There was a moment of startled silence, and then Johann spoke again.

"May the Court ask why?"

"The rebels had thrown up a barricade, and His Highness had no information as to whether they had machine guns. If they had had them it would have been sudden death for any of us to attempt the attack. His Highness realized that fact and rather than risk the lives of his men, charged by himself. The rebels had no machine guns, and His Highness's horse leaped the barrier and carried him up the steps."

"And his men?"

"As soon as they saw what His Highness was about, they followed him."

"But His Highness was alone for a short period of time?"

"He was. He held off the entire enemy force until we managed to reach him."

"Were there any officers among the men who attacked His Highness during the period in which he was defending himself?"

"I could not say."

"Were there any officers upon the steps at all?"

"There were. Shortly before we reached His Highness a group of officers made their way into the Cathedral."

"Did you see the Marquisa among them?"

"I was too far away to distinguish faces."

"When you entered the Cathedral did you witness the actual shooting of His Grace, the Archbishop?"

"I did."

"Who shot him?" There was breathless expectancy in the hall.

"One of the officers by the altar. He wore a green uniform tunic."

"When you took the prisoners, which one of them wore a green tunic?"

"The Marquisa Cobentz."

The Duke stepped back, and Michael Karl thought he caught a hint of satisfaction in his voice when he thanked Urich.

And then the lawyer for the defense began his questioning.

"Are there stained glass windows in the Cathedral of Rein?"

"There are."

"There is one of these above the High Altar placed in such a way that the colored light from it falls upon the altar?"

"There is such a window."

"Is green one of the colors in this window?"

"It is."

"Did any among the prisoners wear white tunics?"

"Two of them did."

"Might not that green light from the window have colored a white uniform tunic so that it appeared green?"

"I do not know."

The lawyer thanked him and Urich came back to take his place by Michael Karl's side.

"They've got a strong case, Your Highness. This morning I would have sworn that they hadn't a chance but now—well, frankly, I don't know. A drum-head court-martial would have settled things more neatly."

"Then you think that there's a chance he'll go free?"

"There's more than a chance, Your Highness.

Even I would hesitate to convict him on this morning's evidence. They're going to adjourn now until this afternoon."

Michael Karl saw his cousin rise and all the court with him. Johann called out something, and the crowd began filing out of the hall while the King came down to join Michael Karl.

Chapter XV

The Last Of Cobentz And Co. (Continued)

"They've got us, unless something happens. They've most decidedly got us," observed Urlich Karl as he wiped his fingers on the heavily embroidered napkin.

"But why," protested Michael Karl, "did you have to have a trial at all?"

"Because there would be a great many people who would shout 'tyrant' and other unpleasant names at my heels if I didn't allow Cobentz a chance to lie himself out of the mess he's got into. We aren't out of the woods yet, boy. Public opinion is a very queer thing and it behooves us to go slow until we have a firmer backing than we have at present.

"We haven't been officially recognized by either England or America yet, and our merchants are waiting. The country depends on trade and those are the nations with which we trade the most. Should some one raise the cry that we were putting men to death without trial, and America and England withdraw their ministers, our government wouldn't last five days. So Cobentz must have his chance to wriggle and lie and take up our time."

"That's what you call diplomacy, isn't it?" asked Michael Karl.

"It is. And now let's talk about something pleasant. We're going to the Summer Palace after the coronation. Do you care for tennis?"

"I've never played," admitted Michael Karl.

His cousin shook his head. "That won't do, it won't do at all. Johann must take you on. He taught me all I know, which I admit isn't much, is it, Johann?"

"Your Majesty would be a better player if you weren't so reckless," answered the Duke with his lazy smile.

"Always am I reproved for recklessness," sighed the King. "And now I suppose we'll have to drag ourselves back to work. I have to grit my teeth to keep from screaming every time that slimy lawyer says 'Ha.' There ought to be a law against it."

The Hall of Judgment was crowded. Michael Karl wondered how the marshals did get them all into the galleries. Whoever had packed them into the left gallery must have had lessons at a sardine packing plant.

The Lords arose and then seated themselves like a rippling wave of red and blue velvet with ermine and jeweled collars to give it life. Michael Karl was thankful that he wasn't called upon to sweat under one of the heavy robes.

Cobentz appeared under guard, but this time there was a smug, self-satisfied look about him. He knew that things were going his way. Bestowing a wide smile upon either gallery, he took his place. Michael Karl felt a little sick. He saw again those dreadful Cathedral steps and that pitiful red cloaked body by the door. Diplomacy or no diplomacy, Cobentz should have been shot on sight.

The burden of the prosecution rested upon the Duke. Michael Karl turned to look at him. Johann was as languid as ever, regarding the Lords before him through lazy half-closed eyes, but there was something—Johann knew something which might save them after all. Michael Karl wondered if his cousin had noted that air of watchful waiting about Johann. When the Duke looked like that, he was to be trusted absolutely. Michael Karl leaned back with a little sigh of relief. Johann would pull them through.

"Colonel Grimvich," summoned Johann.

The Colonel, spick and span as usual, appeared in the center aisle. Michael Karl hadn't seen him since that meeting in the Square five days before. He appeared as lazy and unconcerned as the Duke.

"Colonel Grimvich, what is your present command?"

"The Fortress of Rein."

"Are these officers among the prisoners now in your charge?" Johann began to read a list of names from the slip of paper the lawyer at his side handed him:

"Karl von Litz, Johann Cappleman, Detrick von Kantmann, Yalitz Talmann, and Wheilham Strappmatz."

"They are. They were brought to me on the afternoon of the fifteenth of this month by a squad of His Majesty's Wolf Guard."

"Since that time have they been allowed to communicate with any one outside the Fortress?"

"They have not."

"Did any one of them insist upon making a statement?"

"Captain von Litz did so."

"What did you do?"

"I summoned witnesses and permitted him to make his statement."

"Is this that statement?" Johann handed the stolid Colonel a typewritten sheet. The Colonel glanced through it.

"It is."

Johann turned to Urlich Karl. "If Your Majesty pleases I will read this statement sworn to by Captain von Litz."

"His Grace will read it," answered Urlich Karl.

"I swear upon the honour of my House that the following statement is a true account of the happenings on the thirteenth, fourteenth and fifteenth days of this month.

"Upon the afternoon of the thirteenth I was summoned to the home of His Excellency, Count Kafner, and there I met the Marquisa and other noblemen. I know the Marquisa well and recognized him at once.

"His Excellency inquired into my financial condition and informed me that a serious accusation had been made against me, but for my family's sake he had called an informal board of inquiry instead of a court-martial. I pleaded ignorance as indeed I had no idea of the plot against me.

"He then informed me that the accounts of

my regiment, which in part I am responsible
for, were irregular. I was very much alarmed,
for I and no other had control of them and
there was no way of proving my innocence.

"The proof was very strong against me, and
I had no witnesses. However, His Excellency
seemed to believe in me and conceded that
there might be some mistake. The Marquisa
Cobentz argued in my favor, and His Excellency decided to permit me the benefit of the
doubt. He gave me instructions to report to
his headquarters the following morning.

"I returned to my quarters, but I was
puzzled for my Colonel had not been present
at the meeting, and I knew that such a
matter, a loss of regimental funds, would be
his affair more than His Excellency's. Because this seemed very strange to me, I went
to my Colonel with the whole story. He was
very much surprised and told me that there
was nothing at all wrong with my accounts,
having the books brought to prove it.

"My Colonel couldn't understand His Excellency's motive and ordered me to return
the following morning after I had seen
His Excellency. In the morning I again found
the Marquisa Cobentz with His Excellency.
There was another man there whom they addressed as Kellermann and who seemed very
ill at ease.

"It was then that the Marquisa told me that
Michael Karl, the late Crown Prince, had
been murdered by the bandit known as Black
Stefan, the Werewolf, just as His Royal High-

ness, Urlich Karl, was killed last year. At the same time, he informed me that Black Stefan had gathered an army of mercenaries and was planning to aid the Communists of the south in a revolt.

"Kellerman, it appeared, was a former worker for Black Stefan and had betrayed his plans. The Marquisa said that as heir apparent to the throne it was his duty to lead an army against Black Stefan and the Communists. He hinted that the irregularities in my funds would be overlooked if I would talk my Colonel into supporting him.

"I agreed and returned to tell my Colonel. He ordered me to fall in with the Marquisa's plans. The Marquisa made me his aide-de-camp.

"On the night of the fifteenth His Grace, the Duke Johann, attacked and took us by surprise. Our men were beaten back from the bridge and the New Town. At dawn His Majesty's forces took the Fortress. The Marquisa and a small company of officers, of which I was one, took possession of the Cathedral Square. The Marquisa believed that if we kept the reinforcements from reaching His Majesty in the Fortress we could yet win back all we had lost.

"When His Highness attacked us, the Marquisa and his officers slipped inside the Cathedral. His Grace, the Archbishop, was already there. He begged us to leave as our presence might induce the attackers to turn guns upon the Cathedral.

"The Marquisa seemed very much disturbed, and as we gathered at the altar, demanded of each of us what he should do. Two of us counseled him to surrender, but the very thought of doing so drove him into a rage inspired by fear. His Grace had remained by the door. All at once he threw down the bar and pulled it open.

"His Highness stepped inside followed by his men. The sight appeared to drive the Marquisa almost insane with fear. He raised his revolver before any one could prevent and shot towards the door. Whether the shot was meant for His Highness or His Grace I do not know.

"When His Highness called upon us to surrender the second time, we overpowered the Marquisa and advanced to receive His Highness's terms.

"This I swear to be a true account of what happened in the Cathedral. I am making this statement in spite of the warnings of Colonel Grimvich and in the presence of witnesses.

"(signed) KARL VON LITZ."

"This is the statement made before you, Colonel Grimvich?" asked Johann again as he finished reading.

"It is."

"Thank you, Colonel. Does the Defense desire to question the witness?"

"We do."

"Colonel Grimvich, before you accepted command of His Majesty's Foreign Legion, what position did you hold?"

"I had the commission of Brigadier General in the Republic of San Pedro."

"Are you what is known as a soldier of fortune?"

"Since the defeat of the White Army of Russia I have been a professional soldier."

"As a professional soldier, your services are sold to the highest bidder?"

"I am loyal to the man who pays me, of course."

"Did you, before you accepted service under His Majesty, approach the Marquisa Cobentz for a commission?"

"The Marquisa made me an offer before I came to Morvania."

"Did you accept it?"

"I did not. I did not care for the proposition he made me."

"So you accepted His Majesty's commission?"

"I did."

"Did you, while fighting in South America, learn various methods of teaching unruly prisoners to answer your questions?"

"I have never used torture or any other methods of coercion with prisoners."

"But you know of such methods," persisted the lawyer.

"Any man in my profession does."

"This statement was made in the presence of five witnesses?"

"It was."

"Why is it that all five witnesses are officers

either in the Foreign Legion or in other regiments of His Majesty's army?"

"When the prisoner desired to make a statement, I summoned the five nearest officers as witnesses."

"That is all, Colonel Grimvich."

The Lords were stirring restlessly in their seats, and Cobentz's smile grew wider with every question. The Defense was devilishly clever, thought Michael Karl. If they, the Royalists, should lose, their prestige would be gone forever, with Cobentz and his lawyer making them out a bunch of torturers and liars. Michael Karl understood what Urlich Karl had said at lunch for the first time.

They must win their case and win it not on the battlefield. The time for that was past. But win it in the Court so that the power which Cobentz represented would be broken and discredited forever. A legal victory would have more weight in the outer world than a hundred charges in the Cathedral Square.

The five witnesses of the prisoner's statement were summoned and gave brief testimony, and then the prisoner himself was brought in. He was a slim little chap with a smudge of black mustache on his upper lip and the carriage of a horseman. He repeated his statement and denied emphatically that Grimvich had used any force in obtaining the statement or that he had been bribed. His Colonel appeared to corroborate the story of the missing funds.

It was growing dark and the footmen had turned on the concealed lights in the ceiling of the hall. Michael Karl shifted in his seat trying to ease his

stiffness and wondered how the King could sit
there so alert and still. Urich had warned him that
it might last until midnight for there could be no
more recesses. Urich, himself, was sitting on the
steps behind Michael Karl. No aide-de-camp could
stand at attention through all those hours.

Johann was taking frequent sips of water from a
glass on the table, and his lazy voice was growing husky. Every once in a while a chair in the
galleries would creak as some one shifted his
weight.

"I summon the Marquisa Cobentz," said Johann
hoarsely at last. There was a sudden tension in the
air. Cobentz would have a lot, a great lot to explain.

Cobentz remained seated. His lawyer arose and
for the first time he was uncertain in manner.

"The Defense refuses to testify," he answered
slowly. Urich reached up and clutched Michael
Karl's arm.

"We've got them," he said with a little crow of
pure delight. "We've got them."

The King leaned forward. "Your refusal to
testify, although allowed by law, may harm your
case," he warned.

"He's giving him every chance," Urich whispered.

Cobentz looked uneasy, but his lips still smiled
stonily. He shook his head at the black gowned
lawyer.

"We still refuse, Your Majesty," the lawyer answered, "but we thank Your Majesty for your gra-
ciousness in warning us," he added and there was
reluctant admiration in his voice.

"Are there any more witnesses to be called, Your Grace?" asked the King.

"Two, Your Majesty."

Michael Karl sat up. There was a note in Johann's tired voice— Was he going to spring the surprise that his bearing had hinted at all day? The others in the hall seemed to feel it too, and Cobentz straightened in his chair while his lawyer's wigged head went up like a hound's on the scent.

"Heinrich Gottham," Johann called. A youngster in a wolfhead tunic stepped confidently forward. Michael Karl recognized him as the wolfman who had brought him the Royal Standard just before the taking of the Cathedral.

"In what capacity were you present at the taking of the Cathedral?"

"His Majesty sent me with a message to His Highness. I joined His Highness's command."

"How were the officers in the Cathedral armed when they surrendered?"

"With sabers."

"Did any of them carry a revolver like this?" Johann picked up a long-barreled gun from the table behind him.

The wolfman shook his head. "No. They had sabers and that was all."

"Were there any other arms found in the Cathedral after the surrender?"

"Yes. One of the officers told us that when he and the others overpowered Cobentz they had dropped his revolver by the altar. We later found it there."

"Is this the gun?" Again Johann held out the revolver.

The wolfman looked at it. "It is."

"Will you swear to that?"

"Yes. The gun had a small red streak, near the grip, on the barrel."

"When Cobentz was surrendered by his men, was he armed?"

"No. They had bound him."

"Does the Defense desire to question the witness?"

The lawyer at the table shook his head.

"Professor Rudolph Stadlitz."

A small, stooped man who short-sightedly blinked at the world through thick glasses shambled forward.

"What is your position in Rein, Professor Stadlitz?"

"I have charge of the Police Laboratories."

"An hour ago you sent me a message saying that you had some important evidence. Will you give it now?"

The Professor began in his thin, cold voice. "The bullet which killed His Grace was fired from that gun."

There was a distant rumble like the sea. People in the backs of the galleries were standing to see and hear the better.

"Every bullet that is fired bears the signature of the gun which fired it. The bullet taken from the body bears the signature of that gun. Another bullet was fired from it this morning and compared with the one which killed, and the marks on their sides were identical."

"Were there any finger prints on the gun?"

"There were many. Around the barrel was a group of confused and smeared prints but on the butt there were two very fine ones."

"Whose prints are they?"

"The prisoner's."

"Does the Defense desire to question?"

Again the lawyer shook his head. He looked decidedly unhappy, and Cobentz's brazen confidence had quite disappeared.

Johann turned to the throne. "There are no more witnesses, Your Majesty."

"We have them," exulted Urich in a whisper. "We have them on toast and they know it. Look at Cobentz."

Michael Karl looked. The sometime revolutionary leader had slumped in his chair like a pillow whose plump feather stuffing had leaked away. His face was as greenish-yellow as it was when the Cathedral surrendered.

"The Defense may speak," ordered the King.

"They'll make a try of it," prophesied Urich. "But they're done and they know it."

The lawyer for the Defense did make an elegant speech. But for the testimony of the Professor which he could not explain away, he might have won.

Johann for the Crown made no long speech but contented himself with repeating the evidence of the Crown point by point. When he had finished, he turned to the table and sat down for the first time in hours. The King arose and, stepping down, took the peeled willow wand from the table.

"My Lords," his voice was very clear, "what is

your verdict?"

Reading from a large book he called them one by
one, beginning with the eldest and ending with the
youngest. One after another they arose and, plac-
ing their hands over their hearts, answered: "Guilty by my honor!"

As the steady "Guilty" rang out, Cobentz
writhed in pure fear. His pasty face was such a
nasty sight that even his own counsel turned from
him in disgust.

At last the youngest Lord seated himself again
among his billowing robes. The King hesitated and
then asked again, "Do you declare, My Lords, that
this man is guilty?"

With one voice the Lords answered, "We judge
that he is."

The King stepped back up on the dais holding
aloft the willow wand. Then he snapped it cleanly.
The hall was so quiet that the popping snap reechoed faintly. And then there was a great sigh as
if every one beneath that vaulted roof had
breathed deeply once.

"As in the days of old when the Duke's Justice
sat beneath the tree, so now do we break the
willow wand, for the protection of a pleader for
justice is no longer yours. Your fellow Lords have
judged you guilty of treason against our person
and foul murder. Thus on the twenty-fifth day of
this month you shall be taken forth and hanged by
the neck until you are dead and—May God have
mercy on your soul!"

Cobentz lurched to his feet and stood swaying,
then with a dreadful yammering cry he fell forward into the arms of his guards and they, stagger-
ing a bit under his weight, took him away.

Chapter XVI

Michael Karl Attends A Coronation

"Thanks to His Grace the revolutionists are distinctly in the soup," exulted Urich as he watched Michael Karl consume a late but very hearty breakfast. Urich was a great deal more than an ordinary aide-de-camp. Since the hour when the King had called him into the forest hut and presented Michael Karl as his future commander, he had made himself guide, guard, and, best of all, friend.

Michael Karl thought that without Urich to coach him he would never have been prepared for this day's duties. For what they had fought and schemed for had come at last, and this was the morning of Urlich Karl's coronation day. Michael Karl ate a piece of buttered toast thoughtfully.

"Then we have succeeded?"

"The American Minister and the Representative of the Throne of Great Britain will attend the services in the Cathedral and present their credentials at the first audience to-night. We are, to borrow one of His Majesty's American expressions, decidedly sitting pretty."

"I shivered in my shoes before Johann sprung his surprise," admitted Michael Karl playing with his orange peel, an old trick of his. When he caught himself doing it he looked out of the long window with a trace of a frown. The last time he had done that was in the house on the Pala Horn when he was just a fugitive and a secretary and Ericson was—Ericson, not a remote and sometimes rather terrifying person whom one called "His Majesty." Michael Karl sighed and dropped his napkin on the table.

"Well," he turned to Urich, "what is the bad news? What part in this show am I slated for?"

Urich stood up and brushed the wrinkles out of his tunic with a careful hand. He had a passion for being neat. "I thought," he answered slowly with a mischievous gleam in his brown eyes, "that the Chamberlain informed Your Highness yesterday of your role."

Michael Karl rumpled up the smoothness of his hair with an impatient hand. "He mentioned some rot about my wearing armor. I'm not going to wear anything that I have to use a can opener to get out of and that's flat."

Before Urich could answer, one of the powdered footmen, a ghost of the impressive but vanished Kanda, opened the door with polished smoothness and announced in his low voice:

"His Excellency, the Chamberlain, with His Highness's coronation robes."

Urich winked at the worried Michael Karl as the fat little man, a Jan of the nobility, entered with fussy pomp, a small train of footmen and at least one valet in his wake. He bowed very low to

Michael Karl, favored Urich, whom he disapproved of, with a brief nod, and gave a stream of orders as to how his helpers' precious loads were to be disposed of.

"If Your Highness will be so kind," he said at last to Michael Karl. The valet at his signal held up a suit of soft white doeskin made to fit tight to the body. Michael Karl stared at it in bewilderment, he had no idea that he was to be officially introduced to Rein as a sort of an Indian. But that wasn't the worst of it.

In spite of all his protests, over the leather jerkin and leggings went fine chain mail, supple as silk and light of weight. Golden spurs were snapped on his heels and a silken surcoat dropped over his head to be fastened with clasps of gold on the shoulders. Last of all, Urich girded him with a jewel-studded sword belt whose sheath contained the ponderous two-handed weapon of the Middle Ages.

"Well," Urich stepped back to survey their handiwork, "I must say that you make a romantic figure. Here," he took Michael Karl by the arm and led him over to face the full-length mirror on the dressing room wall, "take a look at yourself, Sir Gareth."

Michael Karl looked. It was as if one of the recumbent figures in the Cathedral, who marked the tombs of the crusading knights, had come to life. Only, thank goodness, his chain mail was decidedly lighter. He hoped frantically that it wasn't going to be a hot day.

Thinking of that possibility, Michael Karl turned to his aide-de-camp.

"I hope," he said viciously, "that you're doomed to something like this too." He indicated the mail and surcoat weighted down with his sword.

Urich lost his grin. "I am," he said dismally as he departed to dress.

Michael Karl paced nervously back and forth, leaving long scratches on the polished floor as he went. For five hundred years or more the Princes of his House had left similar scratches on the floor of that room in Rein Castle. He was slowly but surely losing what little nerve he possessed.

He stepped to the balcony window-door and looked down upon the city. The color of flags, flowers and banners flashed through the darkness of the centuries-old buildings. Rein was clad in her gala dress to-day. Even though it was yet very early, he could see the mass of moving heads struggling for places along the Avenue of the Duke where the coronation procession was to pass on its way to the Cathedral.

This then was the end of adventuring. After Urlich Karl received his crown, he, Michael Karl, would be free to go. But somehow he no longer desired to leave Rein's frowning Fortress and crooked streets. He watched the scene below a bit wistfully.

"Your Highness is ready?"

Michael Karl turned a bit stiffly on account of his mail. Urich stood within the doorway. Like Michael Karl he wore leather leggings and a leather shirt covered with a short coat of mail. A short sword and dagger hung from his metal studded belt and a smooth helmet covered his head. He might have been an illustration out of

Quentin Durward. Resting on his hip he carried a great visored helmet with three plumes, yellow, red, and black, waving from its crest.

"I don't have to wear that too, do I?" demanded Michael Karl in some dismay, surveying the helmet.

Urich laughed. "No, I have to carry it. It's just for show. The Court is waiting, Your Highness," he ended formally.

Michael Karl stepped into the corridor. There was a glittering company of dress uniforms which swayed like a giant garden of flowers at his coming and then he was going down the grand staircase.

The inner courtyard was choked with state carriages and mounted troopers, but at his arrival some small space was cleared about a great black horse with the broad back and heavy heels of the medieval war horse. It paced solemnly back and forth, the silver cloth of its caparisons fluttering in the breeze, quite dwarfing the soldier who led it.

Michael Karl mounted awkwardly with the assistance of Urich and another officer he had never seen before. Evidently his mounting was the signal for departure, as the muddle in the courtyard straightened itself out and part of it disappeared through the outer gate.

Far below, Michael Karl could hear the silvery call of a bugle. The march had begun. He wondered just where Urlich Karl was, and then he remembered that the King was to follow later.

The cavalry troop moved off followed by several

carriages and then Urich, also mounted, spurred up to his side.

"—Next"—was all Michael Karl could hear. He nodded and shook his reins. The horse understood and at a dignified pace followed the last carriage.

They passed between the saluting sentries of the inner and outer gates and found themselves at the top of the long Avenue. The street was packed except for a lane of half its width which the police had difficulty in keeping open. The population of Rein seemed to have trebled overnight.

The war horse arched his neck and trotted sideways. He at least was enjoying himself. Michael Karl stared straight ahead at the powdered footmen on the coach before him. He just didn't dare look at the crowd.

They were shouting now: "The Prince! Michael Karl! Long live the Prince!"

A yellow rose fell, its thorns caught on the silver saddle cloth so that the blossom bobbed along at his knee. He reached down and retrieved it. A yellow rose, the crest of the heir to the throne. It might be an omen. He tucked it in the buckle of his sword belt.

The ride was a short one. Already the troop of cavalry had taken its place in the Cathedral Square. Michael Karl stared at the steps. He half imagined he could see the blood-stained barricade and the dreadful litter on the steps beyond.

Dismounting stiffly while Urich held his stirrup he turned to the crimson carpet which wound its fat length up the steps. Now that he was closer there were still grim traces of the battle to be seen.

The saints around the carven doorway were chipped and battered. Saint Michael, whose niche
had so well protected him in the fight, had lost a
toe and half of his stone sword was missing.

Inside the Cathedral the roof arched high above
his head, dim and cool. There was a murmur like
the distant sound of the sea and thousands of
candles gave light to a burnished tapestry of
bright uniforms and court dresses.

To the right of the High Altar stood a vacant
throne newly erected where the King would take
his seat after his coronation. Michael Karl bent
knee before the altar and then took his place to the
right of the throne on the second step of the dais.

Somewhere a chant had begun, and at last the
newly appointed Archbishop arrived. Michael
Karl discovered that he could lean upon his
sword. He hoped that Urlich Karl wouldn't keep
them waiting long. A rising roar from the Square
interrupted the priests at the altar. Michael Karl
straightened.

Down the center aisle, their somber green and
their wolfskin cloaks a contrast to the uniforms
around them, came a detachment of the Wolf
Guard. A party of high officers followed them.
Michael Karl caught a glimpse of the scarred face
of Colonel Grimvich.

And then—alone—came the King.

Michael Karl leaned forward. His cousin's face
was white. There was a grim line about his jaw,
but he came confidently, almost triumphantly. He
had won.

There was silence in the Cathedral now. The
faint clink of Michael Karl's mail as he moved in-

voluntarily seemed like the clank of a great chain.

The archbishop moved forward.

"Who cometh to the High Altar of the Cathedral of Rein?" he asked and his words echoed down the aisle.

"He who is to be crowned," answered Urlich Karl. He still stood alone, the center of attention for all that throng.

An officer stepped from the crowd. Michael Karl recognized the Duke beneath the gold lace and crimson.

"He who is to be crowned must be the rightful heir. Who speaks for you?"

"I answer!" cried the Duke.

"Is this the rightful heir to the throne, who will hold it as the kings have held it for half a thousand years?"

"He is and thus will he hold it. By the honor of my line do I swear my words to be true."

"What is thy name, my son?" The Archbishop turned to Urlich Karl and the Duke stepped back.

"Urlich Karl."

"Urlich Karl, do you now swear that you shall govern this land with the best that is in you, that you will serve it while life is in you, that all that is yours will also belong to it, and that you will never forsake it while you live?"

There was a moment of silence and then Urlich Karl's voice rang out with a clearness that thrilled.

"I do so swear. I belong to Morvania!"

"Then, Urlich Karl, advance to the altar and receive, as a symbol of thy pledge, the Crown of the Kings."

From the center of the High Altar the Archbishop lifted something that blazed with a glorious light and color of its own and, as Urlich Karl knelt on the cushion before him, he stooped and placed it on the King's dark head. Urlich Karl arose and turned to face his people.

In an instant every one's sword was out and as it clashed with his neighbor's the shout arose:

"Long live the King!"

When the cheering died down, the Duke Johann advanced, a ponderous sword lying across his arm, the great Sword of State of which he was hereditary bearer. Behind him came another lord with the Scepter and a third with the Mantle.

Urlich Karl accepted them after they were blessed by the Archbishop and then he ascended the throne. Michael Karl glanced at his face as he passed. It was a stiff white mask. Urlich Karl, his friend and companion, was gone, the man on the throne was Urlich Karl the King. Again the cheering burst forth.

Michael Karl wet his dry lips nervously. The time for his part in the proceedings was at hand. He clutched tightly the gauntlet of mail Urich had thrust in his belt and stepped down into the center aisle with Urich at his heels. Somewhere a bugle sounded once.

"His Highness, the Prince of Rein and the Champion of the King." Michael Karl thought that he recognized the droning voice for that of the Chamberlain. He ran his tongue over his dry lips once more, took a firm grip on the gauntlet and then:

"Whosoever declareth that Urlich Karl sitteth wrongfully upon the throne of the Karloffs, him do I declare a liar and do challenge to prove his false and traitorous words upon this, my body. I stand ready!"

Upon the bare stones he tossed the gauntlet. It fell with a crash.

"The Champion stands ready," droned the voice three times. Then there was silence and a page ran to pick up the gauntlet and return it to Michael Karl. He stepped back to his old place.

And then for the first time since he was crowned, the King spoke.

"Let our Lords and Princes do homage for their lands."

"Michael Karl Johann Stefan Rene Eric Marie, Prince and Lord of Rein, First Lord of the Kingdom, approach the throne and do homage for thy lands of Casnov, Urnt, Kelive, Klan, Mal, Snadro, Kor, and Amal," read the voice.

Michael Karl mounted the two steps of the dais and knelt before the King. Into his cousin's cold outstretched hand he put both his own hot ones.

"My Lord and Master, thus do I humbly seek thy favor for my lands"—for a moment he was afraid he had forgotten their names—"of Casnov, Urnt, Kelive, Klan, Mal, Snadro, Kor, and Amal. I do swear to hold them for the Crown against all comers, to support thy person in war and peace, to be loyal to the throne and the heirs of thy body, to pay the duties of a vassal to his Lord. This do I swear upon the honor of my house."

The King touched him lightly on the shoulder with the Sword of State.

"My Lord, your lands are yours by our favor. Go in peace."

Michael Karl backed down. Already the voice was droning out Johann's lands and titles and he was going up to do homage for them. And so it went on. Lord after Lord came and went. Michael Karl was hot and cramped. He had just begun to wonder if he could go on standing much longer when Urich touched him on the elbow.

"Almost over now, Your Highness," he whispered. "You don't have to ride back if you don't wish to, there's a nearer way."

"Lead me to it," Michael Karl hissed back. "I'm all in." He managed to straighten as the King arose and stepped down. He would have to ride back in the state carriage. Obeying Urich's motion Michael Karl stepped to the back of the throne and followed his aide-de-camp through a side door.

"I wouldn't have suggested this," explained Urich as he beckoned up a Rolls Royce which was standing in the deserted side street. "but you look awfully tired, and nobody will notice Your Highness's absence if the King is there."

Michael Karl climbed into the car and sank on the cushions with a sigh of relief. "What time is it?"

"Four o'clock." Urich pushed up his medieval sleeve to consult a very modern wrist watch. "Your Highness will have two hours of rest and time for something to eat before the first audience this evening. To-morrow there is the state banquet given by the Mayor of Rein and the state ball in the evening."

Michael Karl leaned back wearily and closed his eyes. "Who, in his right mind, would ever want to be a Prince?" he asked.

The car stopped and he crawled out. Cheering from below marked the passing of the King. With Urich's help he dodged through a small private doorway and reached his own apartments. His valet was waiting and in no time he was free of the mail.

"There is luncheon on the table, Your Highness," murmured the man respectfully as he bowed himself out.

"Thank goodness. Another half hour and I'd have passed out of sheer starvation. Where are you going, Urich?" he demanded as his aide-de-camp edged towards the door. "You are going to forget etiquette for once and sit down and eat with me. Oh, yes you are! Come on."

So with Urich on the other side of the table he sat down to enjoy the luncheon.

"They did us proud," he said with some satisfaction after surveying the table. "If to-night is anything like this morning I'm going to need this."

His wing of the palace seemed very quiet. Even the city below had quieted down. To-morrow night it would be all over, even the shouting. Urlich Karl would be King and would be off for the Summer Palace in the Mountains. And he—well, perhaps he would be on his way to America. His bargain in the house on the Pala Horn had been for the duration only and—the war was over.

Yes, by to-morrow night he might be free. He smiled a bit wryly. Freedom didn't seem so alluring but he supposed that that was reaction. After all, a fellow couldn't go through a ceremony like that of to-day and not have some of his ideas changed. Morvania might smack of Graustark, but there was something behind it all that was real and worth holding on to.

"I guess," he said tossing his napkin aside, "I'll take your advice about the nap, Urich. Call me when it is time to dress."

The lounge felt very comfortble. He curled up drowsily. Some one shook him violently. It was Urich, his mail tunic exchanged for the glory of a full dress one of the Prince's Own.

"Your Highness must get up at once. We are late. Your Highness's bath is waiting."

The sun had gone, and there was a distinct chill in the air from the open window. Michael Karl made a hurried toilet and held his breath while the valet and Urich fastened his tight dress tunic. His dress saber was belted on, and Urich handed him his gloves and helmet. Urich kept frowning at his watch, reminding Michael Karl of nothing so much as the White Rabbit on his way to the Duchess's tea party.

He was hustled out into the hall, down the staircase and through bowing lines of courtiers to take his place in the throne room on the lower steps of the throne. A moment later the King was announced.

Again he entered alone. Michael Karl remembered what his cousin had once told him, that a throne was a lonely place. All at once he pitied the King. That young man in his silver and white uniform, taking his place on the throne, was only a few years older than he, Michael Karl, but he would never have a real friend nor perhaps a real pleasure. He would always have to be careful of his words, his actions, of whom he surrounded himself with. He was a prisoner of state.

Urich plucked his sleeve in some excitement. "The English Representative Extraordinary and the American Minister have arrived and are waiting to be presented. Our cause is safe."

The Grand Chamberlain appeared like a jack-in-the-box in the doorway.

"His Excellency, the Representative of His Majesty of Great Britain, His Excellency, the American Minister to Morvania!"

A lane appeared as if by magic down the room, and the two quiet men made their way to the steps of the throne where they handed their credentials to Duke Johann in order that he might present them to His Majesty.

Two men, one in evening dress, the other in full court costume, standing there—it marked the end and the success of the Royalist's whole mad adventure. The monarchy of Morvania was firmly established and Michael Karl's job was done.

Michael Karl stirred and looked up at the King's calm face. When would he get his dismissal, he wondered. Meanwhile he listened to the welcoming speech of the King of Morvania.

Chapter XVII

Michael Karl Destroys A Certain Paper—

Michael Karl, Prince of Rein and a host of other useless things, had run away. A sub-lieutenant of the Red Hussars was covering the top of one of the tables on the sidewalk before the Sign of the Rose with the crumbs of his breakfast roll but sub-lieutenants have very little in common with princes.

It had been so ridiculously easy. Jan had been persuaded to produce the uniform which he had been told was to be the base for a very neat joke on His Majesty. Urich had been yawning so widely when, at dawn, the ball was over that it had been easy to persuade him that his master was sleepy too. Then into the uniform and out of the water gate.

He wasn't running away for good, but he did want some time to think things over. The lack of privacy in the Castle had irked him as it never had before. He crumpled his napkin and tossed two of the slightly oval coins, which he had stuffed into his pocket, onto the table. Hoping that was enough (he had no way of knowing the proper price of breakfasts in Rein) he arose and sauntered off.

Here and there a bit of frayed scarlet or yellow cloth still fluttered from a lamp post, but for the most part Rein had returned to its workaday dress and lost its decorations. The coronation with its attendant ceremonies was over. Rein was ruled again by a Karloff as it had been for the last five hundred years. Adventure was done with.

Michael Karl wandered on. For all his weeks of residence in Rein he had never really explored the city. To-day he came out on a crowded square with surprise. Sleek horses and some who were not so sleek stood in rows like army picket lines while now and then some one of their number would be led out and shown off before a little group of loud voiced men. Apart from the horses stood the cattle, the oxen. All manner of fowl squawked and crowed from their stacked cages by the center fountain. The shrill yapping of dogs called attention to them, fastened in packs, quarreling, fighting, snapping at each other and at passers-by.

"Why, Lad!" a familiar voice attracted Michael Karl's attention.

Franz Ultmann was soothing a nervous mare and smiling at Michael Karl over her back.

"Herr Ultmann!"

"Faith, Lad, I'm that glad to see ye. Marthe would have it that ye'd come to all manner o' grief, but we hoped for the best. So ye got through, that was good. And I'll be a-thinkin' that ye had more then a taste of the fightin', now didn't ye, Lad?"

Michael Karl laughed and touched his one scar lightly. "It left its mark. What are you doing here, Herr Ultmann?"

" 'Tis the Spring Fair, Lad. I had orders to sell what I thought best, so I brought the roan mare and two three-year-olds. His Grace will make a pretty penny. See them officers?" He pointed to three men coming down the horse lines. Michael Karl recognized the green coat of a wolfman, the black of his own regiment, and the gray of the Foreign Legion.

"They be a-buyin' for the army, and I'm a-goin' to sell them. Ye're not a-leavin' now, Lad?" For Michael Karl, fearing a meeting with some one who might recognize him, was edging away.

"Well, if ye must be a-goin', Lad, and have the time would ye stop in at the Sign of the Plowman and see Marthe? She worried that bad about ye, Lad."

"Why, of course, and I'll be back here later, Herr Ultmann."

The officers were very close now, and Michael Karl had just time enough to step before the next line of horses. The meeting with Franz Ultmann had cheered him immensely, and he did want to see Marthe.

To reach the opposite side of the square he had to pass the dog market, and he did it slowly. Michael Karl had all his life wanted a dog, something warm and friendly to follow him around and snuggle up of nights. The stiff-legged puppies dancing up and down, barking their challenge to the world, charmed him completely.

"The Dominde wishes a dog? I have some very fine ones," a merchant in a coat of a mountaineer edged forward. Michael Karl shook his head wistfully.

"I guess not."

"Let the Dominde look. Perhaps he will find one
to his taste," urged the man. Michael Karl refused
again but still he lingered. Almost at the end of the
line, lying alone in weary dignity, was the most
beautiful dog Michael Karl had ever seen, a great
snowwhite, Russian wolfhound, its slender nose
buried between its dainty paws.

The dog seemed to take no interest in its sur-
roundings but lay still, not even watching the
people who passed. The merchant hastened up.

"That, Dominde, is a very fine dog. A gentleman
of the mountains trained him for the hunting of
wolves. He said that these kind of dogs were bred
for that in his country. He had a great pack when
he died. The dog is very cheap, Dominde. Men of
our land do not like them, although a shepherd
bought some. They are slow to make friends, these
wolfhounds, but they love a man for life. Eh,
Alexis, is not that true?"

The hound raised his head at the sound of his
name and, ignoring the merchant, looked straight
at Michael Karl. Gravely and with a certain dignity he got to his feet and then, walking up to the
boy, he pushed his nose into the hand Michael
Karl was unconsciously holding out to him. The
plume of his tail wagged once.

"Dominde!" there was a touch of excitement in
the man's voice, "never have I seen him do that. All
others he has not even seen, but you he woos. Will
you take him, Dominde?"

"Your price?" demanded Michael Karl, his eyes
still on those of the dog.

"Dominde, he is yours already. I ask five

gruden."

Michael Karl looked at him in amazement. "But that is preposterous, the dog is worth twenty times as much."

"Dominde, when Alexis has selected you, is it for me to demand the price? For some dogs there is only one master."

Michael Karl looked at him a minute and then nodded. "I understand. But this is what I pay." He pulled his heavy purse out of the breast of his tunic and counted out five bills. "That I think is the fair price."

The merchant's face paled when he saw the amount. "Dominde, you are a prince!" Michael Karl started. "On this I can live for a year. Here," he hunted feverishly through his pockets and at last produced an envelope which he thrust into Michael Karl's hands. "This tells of the ancestors of Alexis. It was found among the papers of the gentleman who bred him."

"Thank you. And should you come across a mate for Alexis bring this card to Herr Franz Ultmann at Coblen." Michael Karl scribbled something on the back of a visiting card which must have belonged to the former owner of the sub-lieutenant's uniform.

"A thousand thanks, Dominde. Alexis will need no leash." The merchant bent and snapped the chain off the wolfhound's collar. Shaking himself the dog stepped daintily after Michael Karl, following closely at his heels as the boy threaded his way through the crowded market.

Michael Karl asked directions and made his way to the Sign of the Plowman.

"I wish to see Madame Ultmann," he told the smiling maid in the inn parlor. Alexis curled up beside his feet, resting his head on Michael Karl's booted feet.

Michael Karl rose as Marthe came in. "Madame Marthe," he exclaimed, "I've come at last to thank you for those sandwiches."

She peered uncertainly at him through the gloom and then: "It's the boy of the roses!" she cried softly.

"Who else would it be, Madame Marthe? Alexis, move over and let the lady sit down. Herr Franz tells me that you've been worrying about my unworthy self, Madame Marthe."

"We did not hear—" said the little lady.

Michael Karl's mouth straightened. "That there was much to be done is my only excuse."

As he turned his head Marthe caught sight of the scar on his cheek.

"Ye've been hurt!"

"Only a scratch. I was very fortunate. Did you come for the coronation, Madame Marthe?"

"Yes. His Grace allowed us places at the best window in his town house. We saw all but the comin' of the Crown Prince; we missed that and were so unhappy. Tell me, do ye know the Crown Prince?"

Michael Karl sighed. "I used to think I did, but I'm beginning to wonder. He's changed—along with others."

Marthe echoed his sigh. "It's always so, Laddie. But there's somethin' a-troublin' ye."

All at once Michael Karl knew the relief of telling some one his doubts and fears. "I'm going away, Madame Marthe, and I don't think that I want to. I'm not sure of anything any more."

"But why, Laddie?"

"I wasn't born in Morvania. I was brought here against my will to take my place and rank. When I came I hated it, I wanted to go back. And then I met him, my kinsman, and, Madame Marthe, I liked it then, but he knows that I didn't at first. And now he hasn't asked me to stay, and my reason for coming is gone and so—I am going away."

"Do ye know that he doesn't want ye?" questioned Marthe gently not asking who the mysterious "he" might be.

"He has said—nothing. And I have given him chances. So this is probably good-by, Madame Marthe."

"And ye would stay gladly if he asked it of ye?"

Michael Karl smiled wistfully down at her. "Need you ask, Madame Marthe? And now let us talk of something else. Herr Franz tells me that he is selling some of the horses. I wish I might buy a sister of Lady Spitfire. The Lady is dead. She was killed in the fighting."

Marthe nodded. "His Grace told us. Franz was that glad she might serve."

And so they talked until Franz came to join them, chuckling over a good bargain.

"Still here, Lad. Now that is good. We shall have dinner together."

"I'm sorry, Herr Ultmann, but I must be going. This is good-by, Madame Marthe," for the second time he kissed her hand. "Good-by, Herr Ultmann, and may your roses find the sun very nourishing.

Come, Alexis," and with a smile and a wave of the hand he left them.

He crossed the Cathedral Square and turned into the Pala Horn. The house where he had lived with Ericson was still there, of course, but there was a change, and a new footman was standing at the door to take the letters from the postman. It wasn't home any more. He passed Duke Johann's town house and then turned back. For the first time it occurred to him that his absence might have caused some worry at the palace.

Slowly, very slowly, he went back to the water gate. The single sentry opened it at his repeating the password and he stood in the outer courtyard. From the central tower the Royal Standard whipped and tore in the stiff breeze. Alexis pressed close to his knee and whined softly.

Michael Karl passed almost unnoticed into the inner courtyard and the tiny garden beyond, made of earth brought up the hill by the wagon load. Alexis showed some interest and would have liked to stay, but Michael Karl opened a door in the wall almost hidden behind a thick stock of ivy. This had been his own discovery, even Urich had no knowledge of it. There was a flight of stairs inside which led to his own apartments.

Up he went with Alexis sniffing behind him and then he was in his own bedroom. His pajamas still lay across the foot of the bed as the valet had placed them hours before. He stepped into the dressing room and sat down on the lounge to pull off his boots, there was no need of ringing for aide-de-camp or valet. His head seemed made of lead it was so heavy, perhaps if he rested for just a second or two— Michael Karl curled up with a sigh. Alexis watched him intently, then he too lay down.

Alexis' barking awakened Michael Karl. He sat up rubbing his eyes somewhat stupidly. Urich stood by the door unable to advance because of Alexis who was snarling before him.

"Alexis, this is a friend, a friend," Michael Karl assured him. The dog looked from Urich to Michael Karl and then without noise he returned to sit by the lounge.

"May I ask where Your Highness has been?" There was cold anger mingled with the relief in Urich's voice.

"I went away," said Michael Karl slowly. He doubted if he could ever make Urich understand why he *had* to get away from the palace that morning.

"We have been searching for Your Highness for hours. His Majesty has been very much alarmed. He sent for Your Highness and we were unable to locate you."

"I am sorry. I had to do it. I will go to His Majesty immediately," answered Michael Karl wearily.

He got up stiffly and walked over to the mirror to smooth his hair. "I'm sorry, Urich," he said again.

Urich bowed formally. He was still angry. Michael Karl leaned wearily against the edge of the dressing table. He wished he had time for a bath and a change. Urich moved forward, it was almost as if he had read Michael Karl's thoughts.

"His Majesty is in conference with some representative of the Merchants' Bank. You will have time to change, I think." He moved about softly, laying out an undress uniform, ringing for the valet. "I informed His Majesty before the dog awakened you that you had returned," he added.

Michael Karl changed quickly. The King might send for him at any moment. Alexis accepted the valet and Urich. They were there to wait upon his master, therefore they were to be tolerated.

The valet went to answer a rap at the door. He admitted an officer of the King's suite.

"His Majesty desires His Highness's presence in the Council Chamber at once."

Michael Karl went out with Urich and Alexis behind him. His riddle was going to be solved. Either Urlich Karl would ask him to stay or— But Michael Karl refused to think of that "or."

Ordering Alexis to stay with Urich outside the door Michael Karl turned and stepped into the room he had once examined from the peephole of the secret passage. The great table still occupied the center of the room but now only one of the conspirator's chairs was filled. Urlich Karl sat at the head of the table where Kafner had sat and tried to make peace between the quarreling factions of his party.

Michael Karl bowed. "Good morning, sire."

"I suppose that there is no use in my asking the reason for your disappearance this morning?" The voice was chillingly remote.

"I had something to think over, I cannot think here, so I went into Rein. I don't think I was recognized." Michael Karl's explanation sounded flat in his ears. Why had Urlich Karl changed? Since the coronation he had been so different.

The King got up slowly and walked to the window. He stood with his back to Michael Karl.

"Do you think that you were altogether wise?" he asked coldly.

"Perhaps not," Michael Karl was stung into speech by his cousin's tone. "But I'm not used to this—this"—he motioned vaguely about him. "I want to be free sometimes."

The King turned. "You want to be free. That is why I summoned you." He crossed to the table and picked up a sheet of heavy looking paper. "Your signature is needed on this."

Michael Karl went over and took it from his hand to read. Suddenly he looked up. "This is an abdication of my rights to the throne?"

The King nodded. "I have arranged for your return to America. I had hoped—but no matter now. You can leave by the end of the week."

Ignoring etiquette, Michael Karl sat down. What he feared was only too true, his cousin didn't want him. For him there would be no journey to the Summer Palace, no more days like those on the Pala Horn, and somehow he had always hoped— Michael Karl picked up the pen.

The "Michael" was firm and clear but the "Karl" sheered off shakily. He was glad he was able to blot it firmly. He pushed the paper across the table.

"I thank Your Majesty for all your kindnesses. Perhaps—perhaps I have enjoyed the past few months more than you know. I shall await your further commands."

He went to the door but with his hand on the

knob he turned. Urlich Karl was standing there holding the paper and—his hand was trembling. Michael Karl spoke before he thought.

"I wish it might have ended differently."

"It is just as well. Kings are always lonely," Urlich Karl was staring down at the paper.

Michael Karl started. "Did you wish it different too?" he asked.

"It doesn't matter now what I wished. You may go."

But Michael Karl *knew*—knew that under the King was Ericson. He didn't know how he got back to the table, floated probably, he seemed light and happy enough to. Was it he, Michael Karl, who twitched that silly paper out of his cousin's hands and tore it with such eager satisfaction?

"Whether you like it or not, Urlich Karl," he said with a little gasp of delight as he flung the pieces on the table, "I'm here to stay."

"Do you mean that?" there was a sharp note in the King's voice. The mask he had worn was breaking.

"Of course, you can't ship me out of here without my consent. If you try it I'll—I'll start a revolution! And then where would you be?"

Urlich Karl laughed joyously. "Right in the front line trench helping you run it, because you're never going to get away from me again, Michael Karl."

Michael Karl gathered the scraps of paper up from the table and stepped solemnly to the window.

"What are you doing?" demanded his cousin.

"Watching one perfectly good abdication go

where it belongs."

"And good riddance to it," added Urlich Karl leaning out beside him to watch the pieces go fluttering down.

"You had me scared," he admitted a moment later. "When you signed that, my heart slid right down to my boot soles and stayed there."

"One would never have known it to see your face. I was clearing out because I thought you didn't want me."

"Didn't want you!" and the way Urlich Karl said it settled all his cousin's doubts forever.

They looked at each other for a moment and then Urlich Karl laughed.

"Now that that's over, and we're through playing at cross purposes how about planning our vacation?"

"Wait until you see what I bought this morning," Michael Karl went to the door and called Alexis.

"Good grief," was Urlich Karl's comment. "Where did you get him?"

"In the animal market. What do you think of him?"

"He's a beauty. And I suppose he's going to share our seat when we go driving?"

"Of course!" replied Michael Karl indignantly and fell to pulling Alexis's long soft ears.

"Of course," agreed Urlich Karl gravely, but he was smiling at the two of them—smiling like Ericson, and Michael Karl was very content.

"His Grace, the Duke Johann," Jan was standing inside of the door.

"You may admit him at once, and, Jan, see that

His Highness's things are packed for removal to the Summer Palace. Well, Johann, we've spoiled a bit of your work."

"And what was that, sire?" asked Johann lazily as he entered.

"Michael Karl has thrown a certain paper through the window after tearing it into small bits. He used to lecture me on being wasteful and untidy, and now here's hours of your work gone to naught."

Johann smiled sleepily. "Not my work, sire. I have secretaries, and they must earn their salt. But I am glad that they had their work for nothing this time. So I will have the pleasure of teaching Your Highness tennis after all?"

"Yes," answered Michael Karl and his eyes were shining.

Chapter XVIII

—And So Puts An End To This Tale

Marthe Ultmann was culling dead blossoms from the hollyhocks by her door when the gate latch clicked. She looked up in some surprise. Visitors were few at the Duke's stock farm.

There was a boy coming up the path. A boy in a white shirt which lacked a button, whose black riding breeches were the worse for long hard wear. But the dog who followed at his heels was an aristocrat of his kind, and the horse whose reins were looped over a picket of the gate was a thoroughbred. The boy was whistling but he stopped as he caught sight of Marthe.

"Madame Marthe!"

She made a stiff little curtsey. "Your Highness is welcome, very welcome," she said with a little gasp.

"So you've found me out, Madame Marthe?" the boy asked.

"But yes."

"Well, it doesn't matter," cried the boy happily. "To you I'm always just Laddie. So forget it,

Madame Marthe. I've come to tell you that I'm going to stay, and I love it!"

"I thought you would, Laddie," said Marthe.